Sara Craven

THE MARRIAGE PROPOSITION

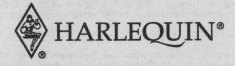

HARLEQUIN®

TORONTO • NEW YORK • LONDON
AMSTERDAM • PARIS • SYDNEY • HAMBURG
STOCKHOLM • ATHENS • TOKYO • MILAN • MADRID
PRAGUE • WARSAW • BUDAPEST • AUCKLAND

ISBN 0-373-12296-9

THE MARRIAGE PROPOSITION

First North American Publication 2003.

CHAPTER ONE

'AND tonight,' Angela said triumphantly, 'we're going to the Waterfront Club.'

Paige, who'd been brushing her hair, stopped and gave her friend a steady look.

'Isn't that Brad Coulter's place?' she queried.

'Well, yes.' Angela picked up a bottle of scent from the dressing table, sniffed it abstractedly and put it down again. 'Is there a problem?'

'I certainly hope not.' Paige paused. 'Unless you're taking your matchmaking talents for a run-out.'

'Brad, my sweet, is an attractive and eligible man, and he's clearly smitten. So where's the harm?'

'You seem to have forgotten one small detail,' Paige said evenly. 'I happen to be a married woman.'

Angela snorted. 'Try reminding your husband of that. Some marriage—when you don't even live in the same country.'

Paige shrugged. 'That's the way it suits us. At least until the divorce comes through,' she added drily.

'Well, there you are,' said Angela.

'However that doesn't mean I'm going to do anything to upset the applecart in the meantime.' Paige resumed work on her hair. 'The grounds will be two years' separation. Clean, tidy and final. And nothing for the scandalmongers to get their teeth into.'

Angela raised her eyebrows. 'Are you claiming that Nick has been equally discreet?'

Paige put the brush down, and began to rub lotion into

5

her hands. 'I've never made any claims on Nick's behalf,' she pointed out. 'He leads his own life.'

'You can say that again.' Angela's tone was waspish. 'If he wasn't prepared to waive his bachelor ways, why on earth did he ask you to marry him?'

'He had his reasons.'

'And why the hell did you agree?'

Paige smiled at her in the mirror. 'I had mine, too.'

'You make it all sound so rational,' Angela grumbled. 'And yet you were only together for—how many weeks?'

'Just over seven, if my memory serves me,' Paige said reflectively.

'It's hardly the kind of thing you forget,' Angela returned, and Paige's lips tightened.

'No. But it's the kind of thing you want to escape from with as little hassle as possible.'

'I suppose so.' Angela frowned. 'On the other hand, in such a brief time you didn't really give it a chance to succeed. Have you thought about that?'

'Believe me, the marriage had failure written into it from day one. But it was a mistake which can be put right, simply and painlessly. However, in the meantime I prefer attractive men—however eligible—to keep well away, until the dust has settled.' Paige replaced the cap on the hand lotion. 'And that includes Brad Coulter.'

'My sweet, you're going home tomorrow, and everyone visits the Waterfront at least once during their stay on St Antoine. It's one of the rules.' Angela's tone was persuasive. 'And it's hardly an intimate dinner *à deux*. Jack and I will be with you, after all.' She paused. 'And I know that Brad's reserved a special table for us.'

'Besides, as you all live and work on St Antoine, you can't really afford to upset him,' Paige supplied resignedly. She pulled a face. 'I don't really have a choice in all this, do I?'

'Now you're making me feel guilty.' Angela glanced at her watch. 'Hell, it's time I was getting ready too.' She squeezed Paige's shoulder. 'And look gorgeous. Competition is fierce at the Waterfront.' She winked cheerfully, and vanished.

As the door closed behind her friend, Paige unpinned her determined smile and leaned forward, resting her elbows on the dressing table and cupping her chin in her hands as she studied herself.

The trouble is, she thought, I'm not actually a competitor, and even if I was I doubt if I'd be battling for Brad Coulter. Or anyone, for that matter.

Because all I really want is my freedom.

Angela had spoken about her brief marriage as if it had been a love match that had somehow come off the rails.

What on earth would she have said if she'd known the truth about Paige's ill-starred foray into matrimony? That it had been nothing more or less than a business deal. A form of words to enable Nick Destry to take his seat on the board of Harrington Holdings.

Her great-grandfather had no doubt thought he was being very clever when he'd made it a legal requirement for only members of the family to serve on the board. But then he'd been born into an era of large families. He had probably expected future generations to be equally fruitful, and equally successful at keeping intruders at bay, she decided objectively.

In his time, too, financing for the company had been easier to obtain. A series of gentlemen's agreements conducted in London clubs. All very cosy and agreeable.

She supposed the deal struck with Nick Destry's merchant bank had been much the same—except that Nick was no gentleman. And cosiness and affability had not been included in his make-up. Nor had fidelity or a sense of decency, she reminded herself tautly.

Apparently he'd made it clear from day one that he was unimpressed by the company's record in recent years, and that he would only negotiate the finance they needed in return for a measure of control. When old Crispin Harrington's ruling on family membership had been pointed out to him, he'd shrugged.

'I'm unmarried and you've got a single daughter,' he'd told Paige's father with cool insouciance. 'We'll have a ceremony to make it legal, then the lady and I can go our separate ways.' A pause. 'I presume divorce won't affect my status on the board?'

And, gasping, Francis Harrington had admitted it wouldn't.

Divorce, Paige thought, was not a contingency that would ever have occurred to her great-grandfather—or not where the Harrington name was concerned, at least. Other people might lead that kind of erratic life, but it could only be deplored and pitied. Certainly never emulated.

He must be spinning in his grave at this very moment, Paige thought, grimacing.

But then her own head had whirled when the scheme had first been tentatively proposed to her.

'I've made it quite clear to Destry that the decision is entirely yours,' her father had said anxiously. 'That there'll be no coercion of any kind and that the entire arrangement must be strictly temporary, leaving you free to get on with your own life after the statutory period.'

Paige had sat very still, her hands folded in her lap. She had looked at her father, but she hadn't seen him. The image in her head had been a very different one—a dark, impatient face, with a high-bridged nose and strong, hard mouth. Not handsome, but with an intrinsic dynamism that surpassed conventional good looks. And charm, when he chose to exert it.

That mouth could soften, she'd thought detachedly.

Twist ruefully into a smile to make your bones melt—if you were susceptible to such things.

A tall, lean body, wide-shouldered and narrow-hipped that looked equally good in City suits and casual gear.

A low voice with a cool drawl, that could also resonate with hidden laughter.

As a package, it couldn't be faulted.

And she hadn't wanted any of it.

She looked at herself, slowly and with consideration. Took in the light brown hair with the elegant blonde highlights, the wide cheekbones, the green eyes with their curling fringe of lashes. The cool, almost tense lines of her mouth.

And he, she thought flatly, hadn't wanted her either. Checkmate. Death to the king.

She should have said no there and then. Every instinct she possessed had screamed at her to curtly refuse to lend herself to something so blatantly opportunist—and medieval.

Her father had expected her to reject the idea. She'd seen it in the defeated slump of his shoulders. The faint greyness which had replaced the usual ruddiness of his complexion. And this had scared her.

She'd said, her voice faltering a little, 'Are you telling me this is the only way you can get the finance you need? That a seat on the board is the price?'

Her father had not met her gaze. 'The bank requires a measure of control for this kind of injection of capital.' He'd sounded as if he was repeating something he'd learned by rote. 'They reserve the right to impose conditions. This is one of them. And, because of Crispin's absurd rule, this is the only way it can be achieved.'

He'd paused. 'But no one is going to make you do this, Paige. It must be your own decision. And if you refuse— well, we'll find our funding elsewhere. Somehow.'

She had said flatly, 'I suspect if it was that simple you'd have done so already. Right?'

There had been another silence, then he'd nodded.

'Then I'll do it.' She had made her tone firm, even positive. 'After all, it's only a form of words. A signature on a different sort of dotted line. And as soon as the legal requirement's been fulfilled we can divorce. End of story.'

Except that it had only been the beginning…

She paused, aware that her heart was thudding suddenly. That she'd allowed herself to stray towards forbidden territory. And that she needed to stop right there.

Restlessly, Paige got up from the dressing stool and walked barefoot across the room, out through the tall glazed doors on to the balcony, the folds of her white silk robe swishing round her long legs as she moved.

The sun was setting, and the Caribbean was pulsing with crimson and gold.

Leaning on the wrought-iron balustrade and staring at the sea, Paige thought, not for the first time, that Jack and Angela's hotel was one of the most idyllic places she'd ever visited. It occupied one of the prime sites on the island, which undoubtedly helped.

She'd met Angela on their first day at convent boarding school, and they'd been friends ever since. While Paige had gone in for magazine journalism, Angela had become a nurse. She'd met Jack when he'd been admitted to her ward with a badly broken leg, and Paige had been astonished when Angela told her, liltingly, a few weeks later, that she was marrying Jack and going back to St Antoine with him to help run the Hotel Les Roches. She was still frankly amazed to see how easily her friend had adapted to her new life.

The hotel had been the home of Jack's family for several generations. With the closure of the sugar plantation which had been their livelihood, his father had begun the work of extension and renovation which would transform the old mansion into accommodation that would combine luxury with informality. And Les Roches had been fabulously successful ever since.

She'd had a wonderful holiday, Paige told herself, but she wouldn't be altogether sorry to go home. These warm tropical nights could be dangerous, and Brad Coulter had been spending far too much time at the hotel lately—even for a close friend of the proprietors.

Anyone else in her position, she thought, would have enjoyed a no-strings flirtation and gone home smiling at the end of it. So why couldn't she?

It couldn't be because she felt obliged to remain faithful to her marriage vows. Nick certainly felt no such compulsion. In fact the whole church ceremony had been a cynical charade, and she couldn't imagine why he'd insisted on it— unless it had been to placate his elderly grandmother who, as well as being his only living relative, was French and a confirmed traditionalist.

Fortunately, she also lived in France, and so would not be aware of how little time her grandson and his bride had actually spent together—even under the same roof. Because, although she would no doubt regard a *mariage de convenance* as a sensible solution to a difficult problem, she would still demand that appearances be maintained.

But Nick was not one for appearances, Paige thought, biting her lip. Nor was he any good at pretending…

She stopped abruptly, aware that this was another strictly no-go area.

She should concentrate on the positive side of the situation, she decided bracingly. Remind herself that the months and weeks of their separation were ticking away to zero. And freedom.

She turned back into her room with a slight shiver.

Sunsets always made her melancholy. And tomorrow it was back to the grindstone.

The dress she chose was a black silky slip with narrow straps, cut cleverly on the bias. She hung a teardrop pearl on a fine gold chain at her throat, and the matching drops in her ears. Her sandals were high-heeled and stylish.

Not to die for, she thought, reviewing herself critically in the full-length mirror. She would never be that. But, all the same, looking good.

The Waterfront had been built on a promontory overlooking St Antoine's most sheltered harbour. It was a large single-storey building, as local regulations demanded, and provided conference facilities, a health club, and its own discreet casino. In addition it had two excellent restaurants, one of them open air with a thatched roof, overlooking the water, with cabaret in the high season and live music for dancing all the year round.

Brad Coulter was waiting for them in the foyer. He was a stockily built man with a ruggedly handsome face. His blue eyes lit up when he saw Paige.

'You look wonderful.' He took her hand and kissed it. 'Angie, have you persuaded her to stay a while longer?'

'Not so far, I'm afraid.' Angela shook her head ruefully. 'She seems determined to catch that plane tomorrow. Some nonsense about having to earn her living.'

'She could do that here.' Brad smiled at her.

'I don't think so.' Paige shook her head, glancing around her, absorbing the ambience of luxury combined with good taste. 'You don't need a PR person. This place clearly sells itself.'

'There are other positions—other roles we could discuss, maybe.' He was still holding her hand, and Paige detached herself gently.

'It's a nice thought, but I'm not really looking at the moment. Thanks.'

'Well, let me at least show you around,' Brad suggested. 'Let you see the layout.'

'Good idea,' Jack said heartily. 'We'll see you in the bar presently.'

And Paige, with murder in her heart, allowed herself to be led away.

In spite of herself, she found she was enjoying the tour. Brad was clearly proud of what he'd achieved, and rightly so. And he had firm ideas about his plans for the future, she realised with frank appreciation.

'Sure I can't tempt you to stay here?' he asked, his eyes searching as he poured them both a drink in his private office.

'Absolutely convinced.' Paige took the glass from him with a murmur of thanks. 'In fact, I'm not sure I shouldn't be recruiting you instead, for Harrington Holdings. We could do with your kind of vision.'

His brows lifted. 'Things not going so well?'

She shrugged. 'We've had a so-so year. More than our fair share of problems.' She paused, pulling a mock-guilty face. 'And, as you can see, I'm a lousy PR girl, because I shouldn't even be talking like this. I ought to be saying that everything in the garden is lovely.'

'Well, there are no journalists present, and your secrets are safe with me.' He looked at her enquiringly. 'So, if your heart's not in it, why do you work in public relations? Maybe the time is right for a change of career.'

'I've already had one. I started out on a women's magazine, working in features.'

'You got tired of that?'

'By no means. I was persuaded that I was needed elsewhere. And my family can be very persuasive.'

'Ah,' he said. 'Then perhaps I should try a little coaxing myself.'

She was aware that he'd moved closer along the big white leather sofa they were sharing.

She stiffened, her hands clasped together in her lap, her whole body language a warning to him not to stray any nearer. She offered him a taut smile. 'I'm really not open to any kind of inducement at the moment. I have problems of my own to sort out.'

'I know you're married,' he said. 'Angie told me. But she also said it hadn't worked out. So that needn't be a barrier. I'm divorced myself, and it isn't the end of the world.' He paused. 'Unless you're still carrying a torch for the guy?'

'Absolutely not.' Her voice sounded clipped and very clear. 'We weren't together long enough to light one.'

'That doesn't mean a thing.' The blue eyes were shrewd. 'Sometimes it can just take one look across a room full of other people.'

Was that how it had been when he saw her? she wondered, and hoped not with all her heart. Because only self-deception lay that way, as she had reason to know.

'For me, it would take far more.' She stared rigidly down at her untouched glass.

'Well, I'm a patient man,' he said. 'I can wait.'

Paige bit her lip. 'Brad, you're really nice...'

'Oh, God,' he said. 'I feel a rejection coming on.'

'But you don't know me—or anything about me other than things that Angie's said.' She attempted a laugh. 'And, I warn you, she's biased.'

'That's precisely why I want you to stay a while longer. To give us both a chance to find out if this thing could be going somewhere.' He paused. 'Paige, I was hit hard when my marriage broke up, and I won't pretend otherwise. But I'm over it now, and ready to move on. When I saw you,

I thought for the first time that this could be the time, the place and the girl.'

She said quietly, 'I'm flattered. In fact, I'm honoured. But the fact is I'm simply not free, personally or professionally, to make any definite plans for the future. Not yet. I really need to sort out my life back in England.'

'I'd like to say—keep me in mind. But the Caribbean's a hell of a long way from Britain.' His expression was wry.

Paige laughed. 'Not since jet planes were invented, surely? I thought the worst part of the journey was actually the ferry trip from Sainte Marie,' she added, wrinkling her nose. 'I'm not a brilliant sailor, so I'm not looking forward to the return journey.'

Brad stared at her. 'You mean you didn't use Hilaire? Then you must. He runs the local air taxi service, which is about as much as our tiny airfield can cope with. I'll call him now.' He rose and went over to his desk. 'What time is your flight? He'll get you there with time to spare.'

'Oh, please,' Paige said, swift alarm rising inside her at the prospect of further damage to her credit card. 'There's no need really. I've got my ferry ticket and—'

'But you'll be much happier with Hilaire,' Brad interrupted firmly, punching in the numbers. 'You won't stay and let me show you a good time—or give you a job—so please let me do this small thing for you. When does your plane leave?'

She told him reluctantly. She didn't wish to be beholden to him, but sometimes it was easier just to give in gracefully rather than go on with an argument she suspected she wouldn't win.

The trouble is, she thought ruefully, I'm not used to receiving kindnesses.

The Harrington clan on the whole tended to be takers rather than givers. And Nick…

Well, Nick gave nothing, she thought, as sudden unwelcome pain twisted inside her.

'That's all arranged,' Brad said cheerfully, replacing the receiver. 'I'll send my car for you at noon to take you to the airstrip.' He studied her, frowning. 'Are you all right? Have I been putting on too much pressure? I don't mean to.'

'No,' Paige assured him quickly. 'Everything's fine. I—I'm very grateful—really.' She stood up. 'Jack and Angie will be wondering where we've got to. Maybe we should join them.'

'Of course,' he said instantly. 'I'm being selfish. It's just so good to have you to myself for a little while.' He came across to her and put his hands gently on her shoulders. 'May I say goodbye now—in private?'

She smiled fleetingly, muttered something acquiescent as he bent towards her. His lips were warm and firm. The kiss was pleasant and not unduly prolonged.

'Well,' Brad said, as he let her go. 'It's a start.'

No, Paige thought with regret. It's not.

She wished so much that it could be otherwise. That his kiss had lit some spark that would have prompted her to accede to his urging and stay. Explore a relationship with him, maybe become half of a couple.

Jack and Angie would have been so pleased—and so smug, she reminded herself wryly.

But it wasn't to be, and that was all there was to it.

'How did it go?' Angie whispered as Paige sat down beside her.

'He's really sweet,' Paige temporised.

'But you're still going back tomorrow.' Angie's face fell. 'Jack said you would.'

'He has wisdom beyond his years.' Paige squeezed her friend's arm affectionately. 'But I'll be back to stay some other time, if you'll have me.'

She glanced around her. The tables, set with pristine white linen and gleaming silverware, were stationed round the edge of a large dance floor. The band, a four-piece combination, were playing quietly, but no one was dancing yet, although all the tables were fully occupied. Soft-footed waiters were moving among the diners, and there was a hum of conversation and laughter punctuated by the popping of corks.

Coloured lights were festooned across the thatched roof, and each table also had a candle burning in a pretty glass shade, surrounded by a garland of bright flowers.

'It's really lovely here,' Paige commented. 'And very crowded. I thought this was the off season.'

'A couple of big yachts docked in the marina this morning. Jack says it's Alain Froyat, who owns a string of European magazines, and Kel Drake, the film producer.' Angie shrugged. 'Apparently there's been a weather warning, so they've decided to play it safe. And their guests have all come ashore to dine and lose some of their accumulated wealth in Brad's casino.'

'A weather warning?' Paige frowned. 'Do you mean a hurricane?'

'Oh, it probably won't be that bad. But we can get the odd tropical storm at this time of year.' She pursed her lips. 'And that might delay your ferry.'

'That's not a problem.' Paige's tone was rueful. 'Apparently I'm going to Sainte Marie in style—courtesy of Brad, and someone called Hilaire.'

'Holy smoke,' said Angie. 'I'm impressed. Hilaire must have had to toss out the odd millionaire to make room for you.'

Their table was in the corner of the restaurant nearest the beach, to take advantage of the breeze from the sea. Only there didn't seem to be one. The air was very warm, and very still. In fact it had almost a brooding quality, Paige thought, watching the reflection of the moon on the calm water. Maybe the skippers on those yachts had known what they were doing when they'd looked for a secure haven. For a moment she was aware of a faint shiver of uneasiness, but dismissed it. She would be halfway home by the time bad weather struck, she told herself resolutely. If indeed it did.

The food was delicious—pumpkin soup followed by red snapper, and a spicy chicken dish served with fragrant rice, all of it accompanied by vintage wines. Dessert was slices of fresh pineapple marinated in liqueur, and a wonderful home-made coconut ice cream.

Brad was an attentive host, keeping the conversation general and light-hearted, and, to Paige's relief, making no further comment about her imminent departure.

Now that the pressure was off, it was turning into a really enjoyable evening, she decided, as coffee and brandy were served.

The band was playing something soft and dreamy, and Jack and Angie got up to dance. Paige watched them slowly circling the floor in each other's arms, Jack smiling adoringly into his wife's eyes and Angie lifting her hand to stroke his cheek.

They've got it right, Paige thought, suppressing a pang of envy so fierce it was almost painful.

'Shall we join them?'

Paige started. Brad was watching her enquiringly, his brow slightly furrowed.

She sent him a bright smile. 'Why not?'

He was a good dancer, holding her lightly and not too closely. As they moved he exchanged greetings with the people at the tables they passed, or acknowledged someone's presence with a smile and a nod.

'You're good at this,' she told him.

His grin was rueful. 'I'm in business, and the rich can

be touchy. You can't afford to ignore anyone. And when someone like Froyat hits town you've no idea who might be travelling with him, so it can be perilous.'

'I bet.' She was smiling as she glanced towards the big table he was indicating. A sea of faces, all animated, chattering to their neighbours. All relaxed and having a good time.

All, that was, except one. A dark face, cool and sardonic, swam out of the crowd. A man who wasn't talking to anyone around him, who was even momentarily oblivious to the young and pretty blonde who was draped across him, her arm round his neck. A man who was staring right at *her,* his eyes narrowed and appraising.

The smile froze on her lips. She felt the breath catch in her throat, the sudden grim thud of her astonished heart against her ribcage.

No, she thought desperately. It can't be. *It can't...*

'Are you all right?' Brad's voice was concerned.

'Yes.' Her voice was hoarse, unlike her own. 'I mean— no. At least...' She paused. 'Do you think we could sit down, please?'

'Of course.' His arm went round her, supporting her, and she was grateful for it as they made their way off the floor. Because her legs were shaking under her.

'Can I get you something?' Brad put her gently into her chair. 'What's wrong? You look as if you've seen a ghost.'

No ghost, she thought. But someone only too real, who was, by some terrible mischance, right here on St Antoine.

She said quickly, 'I think it's the weather.' She fanned herself with her hand. 'It's got so oppressive suddenly.'

She sipped the glass of iced water he poured for her, and assured him that the slight faintness was passing. That she'd be fine if she could just sit quietly for a few minutes. And that she'd really prefer to be on her own.

'There must be people you should be talking to,' she

urged. 'Go and do your social thing while I pull myself together. I feel such a fool...'

'I'd rather not leave you.'

'Then you'll make me feel worse than ever. Please, Brad. I might even go for a quick stroll along the beach—clear my head properly,' she added with determined brightness.

Or I might run away and never be found again...

'Are you sure you'd rather be alone?' He was doubtful—reluctant.

'Absolutely. Anyway, Jack and Angie will be back in a minute.' She smiled at him, willing him to walk away. 'And when you come back I'll be fine again. Rarin' to go, in fact.'

She sounded hyper—like a crazy woman—but it seemed to work. She didn't watch to see what table Brad was heading for, because she didn't want to know.

She drank some more water, staring at the flicker of the candle-flame behind the glass. What was that old saying? 'Speak of the devil and he's sure to appear.' Only a few hours ago she and Angie had talked about Nick Destry—and here he was.

Unless her imagination was playing tricks—had conjured him up to torment her. Her mind was spinning—in overdrive. Could it be that? Had the trauma of the past months caught up with her at last?

All she had to do was look up—look across the room—and she would know for certain if he was real or some hobgoblin of fantasy. Only she didn't dare.

Under cover of the tablecloth, her hands clenched impotently into fists. What the hell was the matter with her? she railed inwardly. Why was she reacting like this? Nick wasn't a mad axe-murderer, out for blood. He was the man she'd married for business reasons and whom she was planning to divorce as soon as it was legal. This was not a problem. Unless she allowed it to be.

It's just shock, she told herself. All these months of studiously avoiding each other, and here they were in the same nightclub on the same small Caribbean island. Just one of life's horrible coincidences.

And her secretly nurtured hope that she might never need to set eyes on him again had always been a non-starter—totally unrealistic.

I should have taken a leaf out of Brad's book, she thought. Smiled and nodded, as if we were passing acquaintances. Instead I let him see me leave the floor in disarray.

She felt her chest tighten, and got to her feet. She hadn't been serious about that walk along the beach, but it suddenly seemed like a good idea. And she wasn't running away, she told herself. Just—regrouping.

Stone steps led down to the sand, bleached silver in the moonlight. Paige paused on the bottom step, slipping off her sandals. The warm night lay on her like a blanket, the palm trees that fringed the crescent of sand unmoving as she walked down to the curling edge of the water. Her breathing was still hurried and shallow. She had to fight to control it. To rein herself in to normality, and acceptance of the fact that fate had played her an unpleasant trick.

Although Nick wouldn't be too pleased to see her either. He was the one who rubbed shoulders with millionaires. She was the wage slave back in England.

But that had been her own choice, she reminded herself restlessly. He'd offered a generous financial settlement in return for her compliance. She need never have worked again. But she'd refused his money.

All through those bitter days she'd kept repeating to herself like a personal mantra, *I want nothing from him. Nothing.*

When she'd reluctantly accepted the job at Harrington Holdings she'd done so at a reduced salary. After all, she was no longer living in London with its enormous rents. Her parents had wanted her to move back into the vast family home, as her brother Toby had done with his wife, but instead she'd found a small one-bedroomed cottage in a neighbouring village, feeling that at least a measure of independence was preferable.

And she'd managed to do some freelance magazine work, keeping the door open for her eventual return.

It had been a seriously difficult year in so many ways, she reflected. Quite apart from her personal wretchedness, her work with the company had been more like damage limitation than public relations. Since Toby had taken over the running of the organisation, following her father's illness, there had been nothing but problems, it seemed. And as for that stupid girl he'd married...

She stopped right there. She was the last person in the world entitled to sneer at anyone's choice of marriage partner after the mess she'd made of her own life.

An incoming wave splashed gently round her bare feet and she shivered slightly. But the chill of the water was nothing in comparison to the ice within her.

She felt blank—numb. But she had to think—decide what to say just in case Nick decided not to keep his distance. She supposed he was a passenger on Alain Froyat's yacht. But he wouldn't be there simply for enjoyment, in spite of the pretty blonde he'd been wearing as a scarf. Without doubt there was some big finance deal going down. Something that would make the Maitland Destry bank ever more profitable, and send Nick's personal wealth soaring even higher.

Not that it was any business of hers, she reminded herself tautly. Neither Nick's financial standing or his latest girlfriend could be allowed to concern her even marginally.

She'd kept her side of the bargain, and now she wanted the whole sorry charade brought to a conclusion.

Closure, she thought, on a marriage that should never have taken place. I must have been out of my mind to lend myself to such a farce.

Her footsteps slowed. It was time she was getting back to the restaurant. She would tell Angie she had a headache and wanted to go back to Les Roches. She certainly didn't want Brad coming to find her and being carried away by the whisper of the waves, the moonlight falling across the water. He might even think she'd gone out on to the beach to lure him on.

She hadn't heard him coming, but then he'd always had the ability to move like a cat.

Yet when she turned he was there, just as she'd known—she'd feared—he would be. Blocking her way. Bringing her to a breathless, tingling halt in front of him. With no means of escape.

He said softly, in that mocking drawl she hated, 'Good evening, Mrs Destry. Or should I say, "Ill met by moonlight, proud Titania"?' And he began to laugh.

CHAPTER TWO

PAIGE stood motionless, hands balled into fists at her sides. Inside she was trembling. On the surface she stared back at him, her chin lifting in unmistakable hostility.

She said coldly, 'Is quoting nonsense at me the best you can do?'

Nick tutted. 'Shakespeare is hardly nonsense, darling. And it seemed quite appropriate, in view of what comes next from Titania herself,' he added reflectively. '"Fairies skip hence. I have foresworn his bed and company."'

She felt hot colour rush into her face, and was glad of the sheltering darkness. She could feel anger starting to build in her. She wanted to scream at him—You dare accuse me of that? You—of all people? But that was a path she could not afford to tread, she thought, taking a deep, calming breath.

She said, 'What are you doing here, Nick?'

'What a coincidence,' he said cordially. 'I was going to ask you exactly the same question. I hope you're here to promote Harrington Holdings for the island development programme. I see you're here tonight with one of the chief movers and shakers,' he added. 'Is your relationship with him business or personal?'

'I don't think you have the slightest right to ask that.'

'Ah, but I have,' Nick said softly. 'For all kinds of reasons. And the fact that I'm your husband is only the least of them.' He paused to allow that to sink in. 'So, please, tell me why you're here.'

'As a matter of fact I'm on holiday.' She controlled her

voice with an effort. 'I presume I'm allowed the occasional break.'

'And Brad Coulter?'

'I met him socially. He's a friend.'

'Ah,' he said. 'And would it be indiscreet to enquire how long this—friendship has had to ripen?'

Paige said defensively, 'What do you mean?'

'I'm asking when you arrived on this little unspoiled paradise.'

She bit her lip. 'About three weeks ago.'

He whistled. 'And all on your salary from Harringtons. Or are you being subsidised—in the name of friendship?'

Paige was startled. Somehow—already—he'd found out that Jack and Angie had offered her cut-price, rock-bottom rates. How the hell had he managed that? she wondered, humiliated. Or was it an educated guess?

She said sharply, 'And if I am? What concern is it of yours?'

'You'll find I'm concerned about a great many things.' He was silent for a moment. 'So you're really not here to drum up trade for the family business?'

'Harringtons don't tender for overseas contracts—particularly ones that are halfway round the world. You should know that.'

He said slowly, 'Well, that's something they may have to reconsider. Tell me, have you been in touch with the office during this extended vacation of yours? Have any faxes or e-mails come thundering across the ocean at you?'

'No,' she said defiantly. 'And I wouldn't expect them to—not when this is my first holiday since...' She hesitated, then said quickly, 'In over a year.'

'Since our honeymoon,' he said. 'Isn't that what you were going to say?'

'Since the trip we were obliged to take after the wedding,' she said brusquely. 'Why call it a ridiculous name?'

'Maybe I'm just a stickler for convention,' he drawled. There was another pause, then, 'You really haven't had any communication with the company?'

'None at all. I decided I wanted a real vacation.' Firmly, she put out of her mind the memory of that last row with Toby, and her decision not to let him know where she was while he considered the ultimatum she'd given him.

'I'd say you'd achieved it. Even down to a little holiday romance.'

'Thank you,' she said tautly. 'You appear to be having a good time yourself.'

'Ah,' Nick said softly. 'But appearances can be deceptive—don't you find?'

Like you deceived me? she thought. When you made me think—just for a brief moment—one night long ago—that maybe this mismatch between us might work after all. That perhaps it could be more than just a business arrangement...

'I think,' she said, 'that what you see is generally what you get.' She moved restively, feeling at a disadvantage, standing there barefoot, with her sandals dangling from her hand. 'Will you excuse me, please? My friends will be wondering where I am. And I'm sure your party will be missing you, too,' she added pointedly.

'You're all consideration.' He sounded amused, as if her inference wasn't lost on him. 'But we really do have things to talk about.'

'Nothing that can't wait a few months,' she said. 'I'll get my lawyer to contact yours.'

'Caribbean holidays and a divorce,' he said meditatively. 'You're going to have an expensive time.'

Suddenly her antennae were alert and sounding an alarm. Because that—almost—sounded like a threat. Didn't it?

Maybe it was something she needed to find out, she

thought, her senses tingling. This confrontation might be galling, but she couldn't end it quite yet.

She paused, choosing her words carefully. 'A quick, no-fault ending of our arrangement? With no property settlement or maintenance involved? Surely not.'

'You don't count the shattering of hopes and dreams?' His tone was mocking. 'The laceration of one's finest feelings?'

Her mouth tightened. 'They weren't included in the deal.' *And if there was any lacerating done, I'm the one left with the scars.*

He said slowly, 'Perhaps I'm looking to renegotiate.'

That insidious trembling had started up again, deep in her gut.

She said quickly and coldly, 'No chance. The original contract stands, and even that isn't for much longer. I want out, Nick, so don't start playing games. I'm not impressed.'

He laughed. 'Tough talk, honey, but talk is cheap. Are you really prepared for a fight?'

'That wasn't part of the arrangement either.' Her heart was beating fiercely, erratically again. The chain round her throat seemed to be tightening, and she put up a hand and tugged at it mechanically, feeling the delicate links biting into her fingers.

He said laconically, 'Call it an afterthought.'

She said huskily, 'Then I recommend you think again.'

His gaze fastened on the nervous movement of her hand. 'I see,' he said, 'that you've taken off your wedding ring.'

'I'm not a hypocrite,' she said. 'I won't—pretend.'

'No,' he said, and his voice was suddenly bleak. 'I'll grant you that.'

There was a brief uneasy silence, then she said, 'Nick, there's no need for this. Our marriage has never existed in any real sense—just on paper. Why make difficulties about ending it?'

He shrugged. 'Let's just say I dislike unfinished business.'

She thought wretchedly, How can you finish something that never began...?

Aloud, she said, 'But you got what you wanted—a seat on the Harrington board.'

'Ah, yes,' he said. 'Courtesy of that incestuous little family arrangement that should have been legally challenged and wound up years ago.' There was an odd, almost angry note in his voice.

She said defensively, 'It's worked perfectly well, up to now.'

'Then why did you have to come to me for finance?' Nick demanded derisively. 'Because your credit had run out elsewhere, my dear wife, and you know it. Harringtons may have been started by a giant, but there are only pygmies left now.'

She said hotly, 'How dare you insult my family?'

'Sometimes the truth hurts, Paige.' He paused. 'So does a bad investment.'

She drew a steadying breath. 'I suggest you take this up with your fellow board members. I'm an employee now, and I really don't want to discuss it any further. As for our non-marriage—that's over. And nothing you can say or do will make the slightest difference.'

'But that's where you're wrong,' Nick said softly. 'Because I haven't finished with you, baby. Not by a long chalk. In fact—' his voice deepened '—I haven't even begun yet.'

They were both standing still, but the space between them seemed to have diminished in some strange way. She could almost feel the warmth of his breath on her cheek. The brush of his body against hers.

Paige made a small inarticulate sound in her throat, then she moved, skirting round him, keeping him at arm's length or more, walking fast, trying not to run.

Trying to maintain a safe distance between them—if there could be such a thing, she thought crazily as she went up the beach, stumbling a little, despising her own clumsiness. Hating him for being its cause.

She didn't look back, but then she didn't have to. She could feel his eyes on her back, burning like ice. Branding her.

Except that she was no possession of his—and she never would be.

'So there you are,' Brad greeted her jovially. 'We were just going to send out a search party.'

'It's a pretty straight beach,' Paige returned as lightly as possible. 'Not many places to get lost.' *Except in some hell of my own making.*

'What's going on?' Angie hissed as Paige took her seat beside her. 'One minute you're dancing with Brad, the next you're out beachcombing.'

'I needed some air,' Paige whispered back. 'I've got a headache.'

'What lousy luck.' Angie was instantly sympathetic. 'Do you want to call it a day?'

'It might be better. I have to finish packing, and I've got a long flight tomorrow.' Out of the corner of her eye, Paige saw Nick come up from the beach. For a moment she thought he was going to come over to their table, and tensed, but he walked straight past without giving any of them a glance. And Angie's attention was fortunately centred on her.

I'm not getting out completely unscathed, Paige thought. But it could be very much worse.

On her way out, a few minutes later, she risked a brief

look at Nick's table to see if her departure had been witnessed, but he appeared to be completely engrossed in his blonde.

Which, Paige told herself vehemently, could only be a relief.

Brad held her hand for a moment longer than necessary as they said goodnight. 'I'll see you tomorrow,' he promised, and she smiled and tried to feel interested and grateful.

But it was impossible. Her mind was in turmoil. Jack and Angie chatted quietly to each other in the front of the car, out of consideration for her headache, and she sat alone in the darkness almost obsessively going over and over the scene on the beach. Asking herself what he could possibly have meant and receiving no answer. At least none that satisfied her, or even offered a modicum of comfort.

But then Nick had always been an enigma, she told herself restively.

She wrapped her arms round her body, shivering. She was shaking inside, aware of a feeling of faint nausea. Of disorientation.

Shock, she thought. That was what it was. He was the last person she'd expected—or wanted—to see. And it was one of life's terrible ironies that they should be on the same small island, in the same nightclub, at the same time.

If they'd spent the evening anywhere else she'd have avoided him, as she'd been doing so successfully all these months. Checking the schedule of his visits to London, or to the company headquarters, and quietly arranging to be elsewhere. Ensuring work took her far away, to the other end of the country, on the infrequent occasions when he was due to stay at the house.

'You could make more of an effort,' Toby had grumbled on the last occasion. 'It means Denise has to entertain him, and he scares her witless.'

That, Paige thought scathingly, mentally reviewing her

sister-in-law's vacant blue eyes and pouting ever-present smile, would not incur a great deal of effort on Nick's part.

She had said crisply, 'She's the wife of the managing director, Toby. It comes with the territory.'

'But she doesn't understand what's going on. Why you're never around.'

And with very good reason, Paige had supplemented silently. Total discretion had been insisted on from both sides when the original deal was struck. However, it was tacitly acknowledged in the family that Toby's wife was an airhead who could gossip for Britain. One whisper of the *raison d'être* for Paige's unconventional marriage and she would be up and running with the story.

She had said, 'Well, I'm sure you can come up with some plausible explanation, brother dear. Because there's no way I'm going to share a roof with Nick just to protect Denise's sensibilities.' She'd paused. 'And Nick would be no more keen to spend time in my company, believe me.'

And she'd spoken no more than the truth. She was sure of it. So why had he sought her out tonight? she asked herself with shaken bewilderment. Implied the things that he had? She'd kept the terms of their agreement meticulously, yet now, with freedom in sight, Nick appeared to be about to chuck a spanner into the works.

Except she wouldn't allow it to happen. And being a member of the Harrington board wasn't necessarily a job for life. Anyone could be voted off. And just because that had never happened, no guarantee was offered that it never would. If the company could just find an alternative source of financing, she thought broodingly, Maitland Destry might be history.

Back at Les Roches, she accepted Angie's concerned offer of paracetamol, and went up to her room.

Most of her packing was actually already done, she thought, looking around her with a critical eye. And what was left could wait until the morning. So she might as well take a shower and get an early night.

She walked over to the dressing table and sat down wearily, pushing back her hair. It was a pale, strained face looking back at her, she realised with a sigh, then tensed, her hand flying to her throat, as she realised her pearl pendant was missing.

She groaned under her breath.

I must have snapped the chain when I was fiddling with it on the beach, she thought, distressed. Something else to hate Nick for.

Sadly, she unhooked the drops from her ears. Pearls were supposed to symbolise tears, weren't they? she thought. Maybe the loss of her necklace was a signal to her not to waste any more time in mourning for the past.

From now on she would look forward, not back. And she'd kickstart the new regime with a good night's sleep, she told herself, biting her lip.

But that was altogether easier said than done. The air in the room was hot and heavy, defeating even the efforts of the ceiling fan, and Paige found herself tossing and turning, trying to find a cool place on the bed, her gown adhering clammily to her skin.

For the first time she was glad to be going home. Nick's arrival had ruined everything, and she could only be thankful that he'd turned up at the end of her holiday rather than the beginning.

'I haven't finished with you.' Those had been his words, so there was every chance that he might come looking for her again. And it was only a fleeting satisfaction to know that he wouldn't find her. Not this time.

St Antoine was not big enough for both of them, she told herself with bitter humour. But back in Britain there would be more places to hide. And backup from the rest of the family. Her father, in particular, had always been uneasy about this unholy alliance, so she could count on his support if Nick started making a nuisance of himself.

But it's all my own fault, she thought bleakly. I should never have got involved in the first place. Should have dismissed the idea of such a marriage as madness. And to hell with family solidarity.

Nor should she have allowed herself to be sweet-talked into taking her current job. She'd been happy where she was. She'd had a life. Whereas now all she seemed to be doing was sorting out one mess after another.

That was two strikes, she reminded herself grimly. She'd have to make damned sure there wasn't a third.

Sighing, Paige turned on to her back and stared up at the ceiling.

She needed to get back into control, and fast. But it was the sheer unexpectedness of the thing that had thrown her. Looking up—and seeing Nick's face in the crowd.

Reminding her, painfully, of the first time she'd ever seen him. It was one of the memories she'd tried so hard to suppress, she thought wretchedly, yet there it was, taunting her. As vivid in her brain as if it had happened yesterday. Or even—tonight.

It had been a hen party. One of the girls on the magazine had just got engaged, and a few of them had arranged to meet in a local wine bar to celebrate the august event. Paige had had some work to finish, so she'd arrived last to find the other three well ahead of her on champagne, flushed, slightly rowdy, and looking for mischief.

'We're scoring the local talent out of ten,' Becky declared loudly. 'So far none of them have risen above two.' She giggled. 'And half of them look as if they couldn't rise at all.'

Paige groaned inwardly. This was clearly not going to be her kind of evening, but she was there, and for Lindsay's sake she was going to make the best of it.

Already their corner table was attracting a certain amount of attention from the bar's predominantly male clientele—some amused, some predatory, and some definitely contemptuous.

And, of those, one in particular stood out. He was at the long bar counter with another man. He was tall, and very dark, impeccable in his City suit. An interesting face, too, all planes and angles, with a cool sardonic mouth. Yet it wasn't his looks, Paige thought, touching the tip of her tongue to suddenly dry lips. Not altogether. There was something about him, not easily defined, which would always draw the eye wherever he was. A sense of power. Of a control that was almost tangible even across the crowded room.

None of which took into account the evident disdain in the hooded glance being aimed at Paige and her companions. But even as she registered what was going on his gaze switched suddenly, making her momentarily the sole focus of his attention, then, as she felt her throat muscles tightening involuntarily, he looked away, his entire stance registering complete and utter indifference.

As she choked back a gasp, Paige felt a nudge from Becky. 'Who's your haughty friend?'

Paige shrugged. 'You tell me.' She made a business of picking up her glass and sipping from it.

'Well, he's the best of a bad bunch.' Becky pulled a face. 'God, what a deathly place.'

'Let's lighten it up, then.' Rhona, blonde and chirpy, filled all their flutes to the brim again. 'On the count of three we empty our glasses, and the last one to finish does a forfeit. How's that?'

Paige groaned inwardly. She couldn't even drink water at speed, so she was bound to lose, but it was clear that if she objected she'd be the only dissenting voice. Easier to go with the flow, she thought resignedly, picking up her glass and waiting for the signal.

Just as she'd expected, she finished last, amid giggles and barracking.

'So what's her forfeit going to be?' Lindsay demanded eagerly. 'Walk round the room without touching the floor? Mime a full strip?'

'Better than that.' Becky's smile was calculating. 'She's going over to Mr Snooty at the bar there, and offer him a tenner for a kiss. That'll teach him to look down his nose at us.'

'Oh, come on,' Paige began, alarmed.

'You have to do it,' Rhona warned, laughing. 'Or we'll make you strip for real.'

Slowly, Paige reached down and extracted a ten-pound note from her bag. Gulping down that champagne had been bad news, she thought detachedly. She was feeling light-headed, and the pulse in her throat seemed to be beating a warning tattoo.

None of the others would even hesitate, and she knew it. They'd be marching over already, to issue the challenge and put him on the spot. But it wasn't her style. Strangers suffocated her with shyness. As for this cold-eyed stranger—well, simply asking him the time would be ordeal enough.

As for anything else...

The best she could hope for was that he'd treat her as a drunken pest and ignore her. The worst-case scenario was that she might actually have to kiss him. Or let him kiss her, she amended quickly.

Do it, she commanded herself, rising to her feet. Get it over with. Then you'll be off the hook and you can go home.

She needed to saunter with purpose, but it was as much as she could do to put one foot in front of the other without tripping. She arranged a smile. Tried to rehearse a few words. But her mind was blank.

Her approach had been noticed, she realised. Her quarry had half turned and was watching her, dark eyes narrowed, mouth unsmiling.

Paige quickened her pace defiantly.

'Hi.' Fright made her voice husky, but maybe that was no bad thing.

His brows lifted. 'Is there something I can do for you?'

'Actually, yes.' She widened her smile and lowered her lashes. She lifted her hand, letting him see the money, crackling the note between restless fingers. 'I'd like to buy a kiss.'

All the neighbouring conversation seemed suddenly to have ceased. The silence that surrounded them simmered with amusement, and an odd tension.

'Really?' He drawled the word, leaning back against the bar. The dark gaze captured hers and held it, something glinting in its depths. Mockery, she realised, and something less easily recognised. 'Only a kiss?' He looked her up and down very slowly, taking in the neat black dress and the matching jacket, the dark tights and low-heeled pumps, and mentally discarding them.

Undressing her, she realised, shocked, with his eyes.

She swallowed, her last vestiges of bravado ebbing away under the calculated insolence of his stare. It was suddenly like one of those awful dreams where you find yourself naked in public, she thought, resisting an impulse to cover herself with her hands. Common sense told her to walk away, but she seemed unable to move.

Helplessly she watched as he reached inside his coat and took out his wallet.

Mesmerised, Paige saw him produce not one but two fifty-pound notes, and hold them up in front of her shocked face.

'A counter-offer,' he said softly. 'But I'll expect a damned sight more than a kiss—darling. So how about it?'

She needed a response, a swift comeback that would be witty, succinct, and ultimately devastating. Something to leave him with egg on his face, and make her the heroine of the moment, walking away victorious.

Instead, she heard the first ripple of laughter from their audience, and at the same moment felt a great wave of heat enveloping her from head to foot as she was overwhelmed and annihilated by the blush of the century.

She found herself immobilised, crucified with embarrassment as the guffaws rose in volume around her, and she heard the jeering *sotto voce* comments that accompanied them.

'In your dreams,' was all she could manage at last, her voice a stranger's, as she forced herself to move. To turn and walk back to the table, trying hard not to run. Attempting to hide her discomfiture. Her humiliation.

At the same time trying to accept that she had no one but herself to blame. That she'd been a total idiot to allow the others to persuade her into such a piece of arrant stupidity. Although the realisation did nothing to calm her feelings or heal the wound to her *amour propre*.

'What happened?' Lindsay's eyes were like saucers. 'What on earth did he say to you?'

Paige shrugged, thrusting the money back into her bag with a shaking hand. Her skin was still burning, her mouth dry.

'Just my luck.' She tried for lightness. 'A complete sense of humour bypass. He—turned me down.'

And for that at least she had to be thankful, she thought, as she contemplated for one shaken second what it might have been like to feel his mouth on hers, even momentarily, and her senses went into sudden overspin.

'Miserable bastard.' Becky turned a rancorous look towards the bar, and the array of grinning faces observing them. 'Oh, come on,' she added impatiently. 'Let's get out of here and find somewhere more interesting.'

Let's just get out of here, Paige amended under her breath. She wanted to be outside, breathing what passed for fresh air. Or finding a convenient corner to die in.

She deliberately didn't look either to the right or to the left as she walked with the others towards the door. The joke was over, and the audience had found other things to occupy them.

But there was always the possibility that *he* might be watching her go, and the very idea made her flesh crawl.

Once on the pavement, she firmly refused to accompany the others to a club Becky knew of, and thankfully hailed a passing cab.

She gave the address of her flat and sank back into the corner, closing her eyes wearily. But the stranger's image was suddenly there, in the darkness behind her eyelids, and she sat up abruptly, smothering a faint gasp.

She couldn't understand why she was so upset. Why she was still shaking and her insides were churning as they were.

She'd behaved like a fool, and he'd treated her with the contempt she probably deserved, but it went no further than that.

So why was she over-reacting like this—when the best thing she could do was put the whole nasty little incident right out of her mind?

I mustn't let it matter any more, she told herself with determination. I'm sure that he'll never give it a second thought—in fact he's probably forgotten about it already. So there's no reason for me to go on torturing myself either.

It was just a chance encounter, that's all. I was in the wrong place at the wrong time, and did a stupid thing. But it's over, and I'll never have to set eyes on him again as long as I live.

The conviction brought a kind of comfort with it.

But, just to be on the safe side, she would make sure that she never, ever set foot in that particular wine bar again, she decided with a small, fierce nod.

And Becky and the others could read what they liked into that.

I was so sure I was safe, Paige thought, staring sightlessly into the darkness, but what did I know? How could I possibly have foreseen what was going to happen? That within a few short weeks he would be back in my life, and no longer a stranger?

With a faint groan, she turned on to her stomach, burying her face in the pillow.

And now here he was again, she thought restlessly. Turning up like a bad penny. Reminding her starkly of all the past humiliations and hurt she'd suffered at his hands. His very presence a threat to her new-won peace of mind.

If she allowed him to be.

I'm going home tomorrow, she thought. And Nick's going back to the yacht, and his friends, and his blonde. And, if I play my cards right, the next time we are obliged to meet we should be divorced, and I'll be free of him for ever.

A reassuring thought to go to sleep on.

She was just finishing breakfast the next morning when Jack appeared on the hotel terrace, looking serious.

'Brad's just rung,' he said. 'Apparently that storm is building up, and Hilaire would like to be on his way before they close the airport at Sainte Marie.'

'No problem. I'm all ready.' Paige hastily downed the last of her coffee and rose.

'But I'm not,' Angela wailed. 'I thought we were going to have a nice leisurely morning together.'

'You still could, but only if Paige is prepared to stay on until the storm blows itself out.' Jack gave her a questioning look. 'You know none of us want you to go.'

'Then now's the ideal time—before I outstay my welcome.' Paige gave Angela a swift hug. 'Life's certainly not dull here. I've never had to outrun a storm before.'

Although it wasn't just the weather she was trying to outfox, she thought as she went upstairs to check her room one last time. She wasn't surprised that warnings were being stepped up. It had been dull since dawn, the sun an orange disc behind a veil of steely cloud. The sea was a grey mirror and in the garden below it was still, the palms hanging their heads, motionless.

Brad was waiting when she came downstairs, and there was a flurry of hugs and goodbyes.

'Come back soon,' Angela called as they drove off.

'I'll second that.' Brad shot her a smiling glance.

She said lightly, 'You couldn't keep me away.'

The car windows were open as they drove to the airstrip, but there wasn't even the hint of a breeze to ease the leaden atmosphere. There was an odd threatening stillness in the air, as if the natural order had been suspended and was waiting for what might come.

Formalities at the strip were brief. Brad stood with her while her bags were being stowed on the small, smart plane waiting on the tarmac.

As he bent to kiss her, she was passive in his embrace.

He released her reluctantly. He said urgently, 'You still have time to change your mind. You could stay.'

She sighed inwardly. 'Brad, I told you—I have to work for my living.'

'And I've told you—I'll give you a job any time you

like.' His voice roughened. 'I'll give you anything you want. Hell, Paige, I don't want to lose you.'

But there was never any question of that, because I never belonged to you in the first place, she thought. And it would never have worked anyway.

She paused, wondering how she could be so certain. Why she knew this kind, successful, attractive man was not for her, when most other women of her acquaintance would have thanked God for him.

He kissed her again, but in farewell and release, and she gave him a final smile and walked up the steps into the aircraft.

There were four seats, all unoccupied.

'Am I the only passenger?' she asked Hilaire, who was already at the controls, making last minute adjustments.

'One more, just.' He sent her a cheerful smile over his shoulder. 'As soon as he's on board we go.'

Paige hesitated, trying to deal with her uneasiness. The strange sense of foreboding that assailed her. 'I suppose it is still safe to fly?'

'You trust old Hilaire, lady.' His tone was reassuring. 'I'll look after you. Get you to Sainte Marie soon as the gentleman comes.' He paused. 'And here he is now.'

At last, Paige thought with relief. The quicker they were off, the better she'd be pleased.

As the newcomer entered the cabin she looked up, her mouth curving in a polite, welcoming smile. Then she stopped, her body suddenly rigid, the breath escaping her lungs in a gasp of pure shock.

Nick Destry said softly, 'Well, what a small world it is.' He slotted himself into the seat in front of her and fastened his seatbelt, then turned to look back at her. His edged smile did not reach his eyes. 'Good morning, darling. Running away again?'

She said between her teeth, 'I am now.'

She fumbled with her own belt, trying desperately to release it. She had to leave—to get off the plane. Because a tropical storm was a welcome alternative to being cooped up with Nick, even for a short flight.

She thought, I can't—I won't endure it...

But as the belt finally gave way she heard the engine start, and the plane began to move, preparing for take-off.

And she knew it was too late.

CHAPTER THREE

PAIGE found her voice. 'What are you doing here?'

'Flying to Sainte Marie,' Nick returned tersely. 'But perhaps it's a trick question.'

'But yesterday you were on board someone's yacht.' Jerkily she refastened her seatbelt.

'Yes.' He shrugged. 'But not as a permanent feature. I always planned to disembark at Sainte Marie and fly back. And I can't afford to hang round in harbour at St Antoine waiting for this storm to pass, so I decided to use Hilaire's taxi service.'

'I'm sure you'll be much missed.' She spoke before she could stop herself, and could have bitten her tongue out. She sounded as if she was jealous, she groaned inwardly.

'Allow me to pay you the same compliment,' Nick drawled. 'I saw Brad Coulter trudging back to his car like a lost soul. Did you console him with a fond farewell?'

'That,' she said curtly, 'is none of your business.'

'And that,' he said, 'is open to debate.' He paused. 'After all, my sweet, we are still married.'

'A technicality,' Paige put in quickly.

'But an important one. So it's natural that I should have—concerns.'

'"Natural" is not a word that I'd ever apply to our relationship,' she said tautly. 'I can't wait to put a stop to the whole ridiculous pretence.'

'Then we have one thing in common at least,' Nick returned coolly. 'In the meantime, is it possible that we might treat each other with a measure of civility? Otherwise a thirty-minute flight is going to seem like eternity.'

It will anyway, Paige thought, biting her lip. Aloud, she said, 'I can do civil. But I won't put up with the kind of wind-up that I was subjected to on the beach last night. No more jokes about getting me back. Is that clearly understood?'

He surveyed her for a moment, then shrugged. 'That's fine with me. Although the temptation was quite irresistible, believe me. But—all joking cancelled. Will that do?'

Paige looked coldly back at him. 'Thank you.'

He gave her a brief nod and turned away, reaching down to the briefcase he'd brought on board with him and extracting a sheaf of papers.

The conversation, it seemed, was over. The contact broken. Which was exactly what she wanted.

Paige found herself confronted by a view of the back of his head. His dark hair was thick and silky, and in need of a cut. But that was one of the few things he was careless about, she thought. A curious lapse in one who normally conducted his life with such precision.

Or was it? After all, how much did she really know about him?

But, again, that was how she wanted it, she reminded herself. This way there would be no intimate details to torment her memory when the final legalities had been completed.

She sat back in her seat, firmly turning her own attention to the rapidly diminishing airfield beneath them while her thoughts continued to run riot. Because it wasn't just a matter of thirty minutes, she thought, an icy fist clenching inside her. It looked as if they were catching the same plane back to Britain, too, and that meant hours. But on a big passenger jet it was unlikely they would be thrust into this kind of unwelcome proximity.

Not, she thought, with a wry twist of her mouth, unless

I'm very unlucky and someone upgrades me to business class.

But good fortune had played little part in their dealings with each other so far, she was forced to admit.

It had been barely a month after their first disastrous encounter in the wine bar when she'd received a call from Toby to say the family equivalent of a three-line whip had been issued for the coming weekend.

'It's not awfully convenient,' she objected, frowning. 'I was thinking of going over to Paris. The magazine's doing a series on the problems of single travellers and—'

'It's not only single travellers who have problems,' Toby interrupted. 'We have a finance guy to entertain, all stops pulled out.' He paused for dramatic emphasis. 'And it's really important that we make a good impression.'

'Is it?' Paige pulled a face at the telephone. 'I don't think I like the sound of this. What's been going on?'

'Nothing for you to worry about,' Toby told her. 'We need some extra financial backup in the short term, and it's not been as easy to raise as we thought. Hence the charm offensive. We want to assure this chap that we're a united family firm, solidly established and totally reliable. Come on, Sis,' he added in a wheedling tone. 'It's not often we ask you to get involved, and you're a member of the board, too.'

'Nominally, yes.' Paige made the concession without pleasure.

She knew what was behind this, of course. Denise had clearly gone into panic mode at the thought of acting as sole hostess, but she would still resent her sister-in-law being brought in to help. Paige would have to perform miracles of tact and diplomacy to ensure the weekend ran smoothly, and prevent Denise retiring in sulky dudgeon to her room with a convenient migraine attack.

I really don't need this, she told herself.

'Paige?' Toby's voice was urgent. 'Dad's relying on you, you know. We all are.'

The emotional blackmail card, Paige recalled bitterly. It had never failed. But if she'd had the remotest idea what form this reliance was going to take she'd have gone to Paris and never returned.

Instead, she'd left work early on Friday and driven down to Priors Hampton. Like a lamb to the slaughter.

Denise, on the other hand, had been behaving like a headless chicken, roaming around the house, giving the staff orders which she rescinded in the next breath.

'So there you are,' she greeted her sister-in-law fretfully. 'He hasn't arrived yet, thank God, but it's all turning into a disaster. I've given him the Blue Room, but Toby says it should have been the South Suite, and I don't know if I've got time to change everything over.' Her mouth went into its habitual pout. 'And Mrs Nixon's been sulking ever since the catering firm arrived. I'm *terrified* that she's going to give notice.'

'Very unlikely,' Paige said briskly, putting down her bag. 'She's always hated cooking for formal dinner parties. And the Blue Room is fine,' she added firmly. 'He's a money man, not visiting royalty.'

Denise tossed her blonde head. 'You wouldn't think so to hear Toby and your father. Everything has to be just so. I asked Toby if I should put flowers in his room, and he nearly bit my head off. Told me I wasn't to bother him with trivia. But how can I know what to do if he won't tell me?'

'It must be very difficult for you,' Paige said soothingly. 'And I'd go ahead with the flowers. If he doesn't like them, his wife probably will.'

'I don't think he's got a wife.' Denise frowned with the effort of remembering. 'He's certainly not bringing her.' A look of horror dawned. 'At least I don't think so. Should I ask Toby? Put extra towels in his bathroom?'

'I think I'd leave things just as they are.' Paige patted her arm. 'I'm sure it will all be perfect.'

'That's easy for you to say,' Denise tossed over her shoulder as she moved off again. 'All you've had to do is show up.'

Paige, who'd crammed an entire day's work into a morning in order to arrive punctually, bit her lip hard. She told herself resolutely that it was not all Denise's fault. She hadn't been trained to run a large house and cope with difficult guests. Yet on her marriage she'd found she was expected to step straight into the shoes of her late mother-in-law, who'd been a charming and competent hostess and who would have sailed serenely through the current situation.

And the fact that Toby was apparently so jumpy was no help at all, she thought frowningly as she unpacked her bag in her room. What on earth was going on?

She unwrapped the dress she was going to wear at dinner from its enveloping tissue and hung it in the wardrobe. It was a simple sheath in heavy cream silk, the neckline demurely brushing her collarbones at the front but plunging daringly at the back. It was clearly designer chic, yet she'd picked it up for little more than a song at her favourite charity shop, where a number of Knightsbridge ladies brought their expensive mistakes. It seemed the previous owner had worn it to a party where she'd had a terminal quarrel with her husband and had wanted to rid herself of a painful reminder.

So, Paige thought, smoothing the silky folds with a wry hand, it's just as well I'm not superstitious.

A tap on the door announced Denise, looking fraught and carrying a bowl of freesias.

'He's just arrived,' she said in a stage whisper. 'Put these in his room for me, Paige. Toby will kill me if I'm not there to welcome him.' She eyed Paige's olive linen pants and collarless white shirt. 'Is that what you're going to wear?'

'That was the plan, yes,' Paige agreed levelly. 'Is something wrong?'

Denise hesitated. 'It may look as if you haven't made much of an effort.'

'Which could be marginally better than trying too hard.'

'Well, I don't know what Toby and your father will say,' Denise said petulantly. 'It's so important this weekend goes well for us all, and you're supposed to be helping.'

'Oh, for God's sake,' Paige said with irritation. 'What a ridiculous fuss. Just who the hell is this guy?'

But Denise had already flitted away, muttering distractedly.

Left alone again, Paige ran a comb through her hair and added a touch of coral lustre to her mouth. She was not, however, prepared to change her clothes. The guest of the year would just have to take her as he found her, she decided with a shrug.

Yet not all Denise's instincts were wrong, Paige thought appreciatively as she let herself into the Blue Room a few minutes later. It was at the back of the house, overlooking the formal garden, and she'd always thought it much the nicest of the guest rooms, especially when filled with late-afternoon sunlight as it was now.

The walls were painted in a soft Wedgwood blue colour, and the curtains and bedcover were in a similar shade, overlaid with the tracery of a delicate floral pattern in pink, dark green and gold. The furniture was in polished rosewood.

Paige set down the freesias with care on the top of the tallboy, then crossed to the window to open it a few inches further. Birds were singing, and she could smell the scent of new-mown grass.

She drew a deep breath of contentment.

If this financial wizard didn't think he was in paradise then there was no hope for him, and Harrington Holdings was better off without him.

As she turned towards the door she heard voices outside, and halted in dismay.

Hell, Toby had brought the newcomer straight upstairs instead of offering him tea in the drawing room as she'd expected. And the last thing she wanted was to be found loitering in his bedroom.

For an absurd moment she contemplated hiding in the bathroom, but common sense reminded her that this was probably the first place the wizard would make for, and would simply make an awkward situation worse.

Far better, she thought, to pass the whole thing off with a smile. After all, she had nothing to apologise for, even though this wasn't the introduction she'd had in mind.

As the door opened she lifted her chin, arranging her features pleasantly.

'We do hope you'll be comfortable here,' Toby was saying in the unctuous tone he sometimes adopted, and which always grated on her.

'Thank you. I'm sure I shall be.' The deep, husky drawl was instantly, shockingly recognisable.

Paige stood, rooted to the spot, her lips parting in a gasp of pure horror and disbelief. But there was no mistake. Not even the hallucination she was silently praying for.

Because standing beside Toby in the doorway, his dark eyes brilliant with amusement, was her tormentor from the wine bar.

'My every need is clearly going to be catered for,' he added silkily, and Paige felt the swift burn of embarrassment over her skin.

Toby was frowning. 'Paige—what on earth are you doing in here?'

'Just checking for Denise that everything's in place.' Her voice sounded as if she was being strangled.

Toby turned to his companion. 'I don't think you've met my sister. Paige—this is Nicholas Destry of Maitland Destry.'

Paige squared her shoulders. Her smile felt as if she'd nailed it there. 'How do you do, Mr Destry?' Keep it polite, keep it formal, and maybe he'll play along, she thought frantically.

'Actually, Miss Harrington, we've met before.' Nicholas Destry was enjoying his own game. He turned to Toby. 'Your sister approached me once over a financial transaction, but it fell through. Something I've always regretted,' he added meditatively.

'Really?' Toby was surprised. 'You never mentioned it, Sis.'

She said, 'I didn't make the connection before—Mr Destry. Something I shall always regret too.'

'Please,' he said, 'call me Nick.' He paused. 'After all, we're practically old friends.'

She longed to tell him to go to hell, with suitable embellishments, but she couldn't. If he was here to do an important deal then she would have to hang in there and endure all the jibes that were coming her way. And she couldn't doubt there'd be plenty, she thought, her heart sinking. Not an opportunity missed to ruffle her feathers, if she was any judge.

She wondered what excuse she could come up with to cut her visit short and return to London, then saw his swift grin and realised he'd read her mind with total accuracy.

She would have to stay and tough it out, she thought with bitter resignation.

'Well—er—Nick, we'll leave you in peace to unpack,' Toby said, breaking the taut silence with an uneasy attempt at joviality. 'Join us in the drawing room when you're ready.'

Nick Destry was still watching Paige, an unholy glint in his eyes. 'You wouldn't like to stay, Miss Harrington—and give me a hand?' He picked up his travel bag and tossed it on to the wide bed.

Somehow he made it sound a perfectly reasonable request. Only Paige picked up and resented the covert innuendo—just as he'd intended, she acknowledged, seething.

'Well, of course,' Toby said with some bewilderment, 'if Paige can be of assistance...'

She sent Nick Destry an inimical glance. She said, coolly and clearly, 'I think my sister-in-law is waiting for me, Mr Destry, but I'll be glad to send our housekeeper to you if you feel you need help unpacking.'

His grin widened. 'I'll struggle through somehow.'

'I'm sure,' Paige said stonily. 'Now, please excuse me.'

Toby caught up with her on the stairs. 'What was all that about? And where did you meet Nick Destry?' he demanded suspiciously.

She shrugged. 'At some City do, I think. Who knows? His memory's clearly much better than mine,' she added lightly.

'Well, you certainly seem to have made an impression.' He was frowning slightly. 'Maybe we can capitalise on that.' He paused. 'You won't forget how important this weekend is for all of us, will you?'

'I doubt I'll get the chance,' Paige returned grimly. 'Everyone seems to be falling over themselves to remind me.' She gave him a sidelong glance. 'What's been going on at Harrington Holdings, Toby? What kind of problem do we have that needs someone like Nick Destry to provide a solution. The whole thing worries me.'

'Well, it needn't,' he said instantly. 'We've had a few

setbacks, I admit, but nothing we can't overcome if we all pull together.'

'You don't feel like describing these ''setbacks'' in detail for me—just so that I know what we're up against?'

'Now isn't really a good time,' he said dismissively. 'And you've never taken a searching interest before in the company's affairs.'

'No,' Paige said slowly. 'And I'm beginning to see that could have been a mistake.'

At the drawing room door, she hesitated. 'Toby, don't rely on me to win over Nick Destry's heart and mind. Please believe that we're never likely to be friends.'

He said heavily, 'But neither can we afford to have him as an enemy. Perhaps you, in turn, should remember that.'

And he walked away, leaving her staring after him, new uneasiness churning in her stomach.

Tea was not the easiest meal Paige had ever sat through, but she had to admit that Nick Destry's company manners seemed impeccable. There were no edged remarks for her to smart under. Instead he talked amusingly and intelligently on a variety of subjects, so that even Denise began to relax a little under the onslaught of his charm.

To hear him you'd think this was simply a social occasion, Paige thought, chewing an inoffensive cucumber sandwich as if it had been constructed from cement. And yet she knew that it wasn't true. That this weekend represented big business. And that she wasn't content merely to serve as decoration.

Perhaps I should have taken more of an interest in the company business, she thought restively. But I've never actually been encouraged to do so. To trespass on what has always been a man's world.

The fact that it was now the twenty-first century had done nothing to alter the entrenched attitudes of the

Harrington males. She was the first girl to be born into the family since old Crispin's time, and she'd been petted and spoiled, and kindly excluded from what was seen as the real business of life—the prime building developments that Harringtons had always specialised in.

The fact that she'd found a job in magazine journalism and established herself as an independent woman had been regarded as some strange aberration.

If we're in serious trouble, Paige thought—and I can't see any other reason for Maitland Destry to become involved—then maybe it's time I made them take me seriously too.

As she reached across to put her empty cup on the table she was suddenly conscious that she was being watched. She glanced up and met Nick Destry's contemplative gaze. There was a faint smile playing around his firm mouth that suggested he found his thoughts pleasant, and an odd, almost primeval shiver rippled down her spine in response.

For a brief moment the laughter and chat in the room faded away to nothing, and Paige was aware of him and nothing but him, as if they were enclosed together in some glass case. Locked in intimacy for all eternity.

She felt her mouth go dry. She moved jerkily, picking up a plate of cake and offering it to her father. Anything—*anything*—to break the spell, she thought almost frantically.

And it occurred to her, with sudden appalling clarity, that, whatever trouble Harringtons might be in, her own most serious problem could be right here in this room.

She hesitated for a long time that evening before changing into the cream dress, then told herself she was being ridiculous. She was dressing for herself, and certainly not for Nick Destry.

She'd completely overreacted downstairs, she realised. She was still too conscious of the humiliation she'd suffered at his hands at their first meeting. That was the only explanation, and it was something she'd have to deal with, given the opportunity.

And she looked good, she thought with a touch of defiance. She'd skilfully softened the rather taut lines of her face with cosmetics, and her newly washed hair was piled on top of her head in a loose topknot, with just a few silky tendrils allowed to hang free.

'You'll do,' she told her reflection with an approving nod.

She went slowly downstairs, and paused outside the drawing room door to take a deep, steadying breath. A good move, as it happened, because the room was empty apart from Nick Destry himself, who was standing by the French windows looking into the garden.

His back was turned to her, and he appeared to be deep in thought. Paige checked instantly, wondering whether she could manage a strategic withdrawal before she was noticed.

Without looking round, he said, 'I seem to be every hostess's worst nightmare—the guest who comes down first.'

'No—no, really.' Paige came unwillingly forward, cursing under her breath. 'I can't think where the others are,' she added, looking round her as if she might find them hiding behind sofas, or under one of the Pembroke tables.

'Holding a council of war somewhere, I imagine.' He turned, the dark gaze sharpening into intensity as it dwelt on her. The formality of dinner jacket and black tie only accentuated his formidable attraction, she recognised reluctantly. But it did nothing to disguise the sheer raw energy of the man, however tightly he kept it leashed. And that was what confused and disturbed her—her conviction that all the elegance and charm was only a façade, and that underneath was pure tiger.

'You haven't been invited to join in their deliberations?' he went on.

'No,' she said. 'Should I?'

'You're a member of the Harrington board.'

'Yes, but that's pretty meaningless in my case,' she said. 'If you're a member of the family there's no escape. Great-grandfather Crispin saw to that.'

He said softly, 'Indeed he did. Does anyone know why?'

'Because he was determined that the company should stay in the hands of his descendants and not be hijacked by outsiders, however rich and powerful.' She paused to allow that to sink in, then offered him a limpid smile. 'Can I get you a drink?'

'Thank you,' he said. 'I'd like a Scotch with a little plain water.'

Paige moved to the side table, where the decanters were placed, and poured a measure of whisky into one of the plain heavy-bottomed glasses, adding a judicious amount of water. She turned to find Nick had crossed the room and was standing just behind her.

'Oh.' She jumped slightly, then steadied herself as she handed him the glass. 'I hope that's all right.'

'It looks fine.' He watched as she poured herself a modest dry sherry. 'What shall we drink to?'

Paige lifted her glass. 'Why not Great-grandfather Crispin?'

'As you wish.' He sounded faintly amused, but he drank. 'You don't find his attitude a little unreasonable—in this day and age?'

'Not particularly,' Paige lied. 'As long as there are Harringtons around, why shouldn't they run their own company? After all, you come here from Maitland Destry. I presume there's still a Maitland?'

'Certainly—the last time I looked. A couple of them.'

'Well, there you are.' Paige took a fortifying sip of

sherry. 'And I'm sure you'll expect your son to take over from you when the time comes.'

He said slowly, 'I suspect that will remain up to my son—if I ever have one.'

'You don't want a family?'

'Some day. But the usual preliminary to that is finding a wife. And so far I've been too busy.'

Paige tutted. 'Careful, Mr Destry. You know what they say about all work and no play.'

He smiled, taking a reflective mouthful of Scotch. 'Oh, I play, Miss Harrington, when—and how—I want.' His eyes wandered over her, slowly, lingeringly, and Paige felt her skin warm under his scrutiny.

She walked hurriedly away to the wide empty fireplace and stood on one side of it, as if she was taking guard. Nick followed her, occupying the opposite position. She'd wanted an opportunity to confront him, and this was clearly it.

She thought, *En garde.*

Aloud, she said, 'Actually, I have to thank you.'

His brows lifted. 'You amaze me,' he drawled. 'Why?'

'For not telling my family the truth about our first meeting.' She allowed herself a rueful smile and a shrug. Offering amends with charm and sincerity, she thought cynically. Wiping the slate clean. 'Not one of my golden memories. And I do apologise for all that girl-power nonsense,' she added quickly. 'I'm afraid we'd had too much to drink.'

'Your companions certainly had.'

Paige's heart skipped a beat. Just how closely had he been watching them? she asked herself.

Her voice took on a slight edge. 'What I'm trying to say is that I don't make a habit of accosting total strangers and asking them to kiss me.'

'It was a first for me, too,' Nick said calmly. 'However—a word of advice. Your success rate might be higher if you didn't wave your money around like a battle flag.' His gaze rested on her parted lips. 'All you really had to do was—ask.'

For a moment the silence between them flared into tension. Then Paige recovered herself.

'Thank you,' she said coldly. 'But I shan't be accepting any more girly dares in the foreseeable future.'

He gave her an unabashed grin. 'And life will be the poorer for it. Remember—all work and no play…'

Paige sipped her sherry as if it was hemlock. And then the door opened and her father came in.

'My dear chap, I'm so sorry. Quite unforgivable to keep you waiting.' Francis Harrington beamed at them. 'I hope Paige has been looking after you?'

'Oh, yes,' Nick Destry said softly. 'I've been well entertained. Thank you.'

'Excellent. Let me freshen your drink. I see we're promised fine weather tomorrow. Did my son mention we have a tennis court? Perhaps you young people might find time for a few sets.'

He chatted on amiably and Paige turned away, thankful that her ordeal seemed to be over at last. But she knew in her heart that it would really only end on Sunday afternoon, when she could put a hundred miles between herself and Hampton Priors—and an even greater distance between herself and Nick Destry.

To Paige's surprise, dinner was served in the smaller family dining room, with its more intimate circular table, and her heart sank when she realised she'd been placed next to Nick.

He held the chair for her, and as she sat down his hand brushed the exposed skin of her back. It was the most fleeting of contacts, yet she felt it in her bones. Knew the tremble of it along her nerve-endings. Her fingers were shaking as she unfolded her napkin.

The *vichyssoise* was excellent, but Paige barely tasted a mouthful. To her relief, Nick spent the first course talking to Denise, seated on his other side. In the past, Paige had been irritated by the sound of her sister-in-law's tinkling laugh, but now she welcomed it, and hoped devoutly that Denise would continue to monopolise his attention for the rest of the meal.

But her hopes were in vain. As the plates were being efficiently changed by the catering staff Nick said softly, 'Relax.'

'I'm fine.'

'You're vibrating like the string section of a philharmonic orchestra.'

She bit her lip, staring down at the plate of poached salmon which had been placed in front of her. 'Don't be ridiculous.'

'If you find this weekend such a problem, why did you agree to come?'

'I had very little choice in the matter.'

'Ah,' he said, meditatively. 'The Harringtons circling the wagons when attack is threatened.'

'We believe in family loyalty, certainly.'

'And just how far are you prepared to let this famous loyalty take you, Miss Harrington? Or may I call you Paige?'

'Once again, I suspect I have little choice.' Paige drank some of the Pouilly Fumé which had been poured into her glass.

'And I suppose that answers both of my questions.' There was an odd flatness in his voice.

She was bracing herself for more interrogation when he suddenly turned back to Denise, reducing her to nervous giggles within seconds.

As Paige picked up her fork she became aware that her father was watching her anxiously across the table. She paused uncertainly, her brows lifting in question, but he looked away and began talking to Toby.

What's going on here? she asked herself restively as she picked at her salmon. She'd been asked to help entertain difficult guests before. It was hardly a new situation. Yet every instinct told her that this occasion was somehow different. That there was a hidden agenda of which only she remained unaware.

Things must be worse than I thought, she told herself unhappily. But why? Harringtons had managed to survive war, peacetime slumps in the building industry, attempted buy-outs and full-blown recessions. So what on earth could have gone so terribly wrong?

When the main course—chicken simmered with shallots in a rich wine sauce—had been served, Nick turned back to her. Instantly she stiffened, but to her surprise he began to chat with impersonal civility about books and the theatre. As these were among her interests too, she was able to respond with reasonable readiness. He had a strong critical capacity, she discovered, and marked opinions, but he didn't seek to impose them. He seemed far more interested in what she felt and thought, and for a little while at least Paige found they were as near to harmony as they were ever likely to be.

All the same it was a relief when the meal ended and she and Denise went off to the drawing room, leaving the men to their brandy and cigars. The preliminaries had been dealt with, she thought, closing the door behind her. Now the main bout could begin.

'I think it's going quite well, don't you?' Denise busied herself pouring coffee. 'But I hope that man's not going to be a regular guest,' she added, frowning.

'You seemed to be getting on with him pretty well.'

'I admit he's gorgeous.' Denise's frown deepened. 'But even when he's talking to you, you don't know what he's thinking—and I hate that. I always know what Toby's thinking,' she added naively. 'Even if I don't like it very much.'

Paige gave a non-committal shrug. 'I just wish I could be a fly on the wall,' she muttered.

'What—and listen to all that boring business stuff?' Denise looked at her as if she'd grown an additional head.

'I have a feeling it could be more critical than that,' Paige said drily. She paused. 'Denise—does Toby never talk to you about what's going on?'

Denise wrinkled her nose. 'Not really. But I don't think things have been going too well. There's this wonderful new designer, Francine Kaye, and when I suggested we should ask her to redo this room he got quite cross with me. Said he wasn't made of bloody money.'

'I see.' Paige looked around. 'I thought you'd had it completely redecorated two years ago.'

'Well, I did. But this look is so old hat now. And it's so important to have just the right background for entertaining. Toby always understood before, but this year he's been talking about nothing but cutting back. I'm sick of hearing it.'

There was real petulance in her tone.

Paige sought to pour oil on troubled waters. 'I really like what you've done with the Blue Room.'

'Do you really?' Denise launched herself into an eager recital of colour charts and fabric suppliers, leaving Paige to wrestle with her own troublous thoughts.

Whatever deal was currently being hammered out, she could only pray it would be enough to save Harringtons. But Nick Destry wasn't her idea of a saviour. More of a predator, seeking what he might devour, she thought, then condemned herself for being over-fanciful.

But she couldn't doubt that he would drive a hard bargain, and Denise might well find all her decorating plans for the Hall put on indefinite hold. She might have to hang on to her current Porsche as well, and wear the same dress twice. A fate worse than death.

She stopped there, feeling slightly ashamed of herself. After all, Toby had not chosen to marry an economist, nor had he ever tried to curb Denise's extravagance—or not until now.

And in some ways I've been just as bad, she thought. Because I've taken Harringtons for granted all my life. The company—this house—has always been my safety net, which makes all my claims of independence look pretty pathetic.

But from now on I'll take nothing on trust, and I need to talk to my father and find out just how bad things really are.

Just for a moment she allowed herself to contemplate the worst-case scenario. That Harringtons might go into receivership and that everything, including this house, might be lost.

That, she thought with cold resolution, could not be allowed to happen. And she would do her utmost to prevent it.

Whatever it takes, she thought. Whatever it takes.

She found herself suddenly and inexplicably remembering that moment earlier, when Nick Destry's fingers had touched her skin. And she felt herself shiver.

CHAPTER FOUR

I SHOULD have known, Paige told herself broodingly as she stared down at the sea. Should have realised what was coming. All the clues were there. Only I didn't—couldn't—believe that such a thing was possible. That they would ever ask me to do—that.

Or that I would agree...

That was and always would be, she thought, the most astonishing part of the whole thing.

Instinct had already been telling her to run. But family duty had kept her in chains.

Time in the drawing room had dragged that night, she remembered, every minute seeming like an hour.

'How much longer are they going to be?' Denise had demanded fretfully, glancing at her narrow gold wristwatch. 'What on earth can they be discussing all this time?'

And Paige, prowling restlessly from one of the drawing rooms to the other, unable to settle, thought, *Survival.*

'For heaven's sake sit down.' Denise rounded on her crossly. 'All this pacing up and down is making me nervous.'

'I'm sorry. I'm a little nervous myself.' Paige paused. 'In fact, I have a slight headache. I think I'll go to bed.'

'Oh, you poor thing,' Denise said instantly. 'Would you like some of my special tablets? They're absolutely amazing—as you know, I used to get the most terrible migraines.'

Paige smiled with an effort. 'A good night's rest is all I need, but thank you.' She hesitated. 'You'll make my apologies to the others?'

'Well, yes.' Denise's acquiescence was reluctant. 'But I don't think Toby will be very pleased. He was relying on you to be nice to Mr Destry.'

'I'm afraid that was always a forlorn hope.' Paige walked to the door.

'But I don't want to be left with him,' Denise wailed.

'Then I'd arrange another quick migraine,' Paige flung over her shoulder. 'Goodnight.'

Up in her room, she undressed and put on her dressing gown, then unpinned and brushed her hair.

The headache was a fiction, but it could quite easily become a reality. The tensions of the evening had really got to her.

But there's nothing I can do, she thought, easing her shoulders under the satin robe, except join in the rejoicing tomorrow if the news is good, or help pick up the pieces if it's bad. Her mind flinched away from that possibility.

It was good to be alone, but the benefits of an early night had suddenly lost their appeal. Her brain was teeming, and sleep was a thousand miles away.

She retrieved pad and pen from her bag and curled up on the window seat, sketching out ideas for future series for the magazine. Some topics never lost their appeal with readers, she thought, but instead of the search for Mr Right, maybe they should explore ways of spotting and banishing Mr Wrong. She could write that herself.

She made a few notes, but her heart wasn't in it, and she laid the pad aside with a sigh, resting her head against the cool glass while she looked down into the moonlit garden.

She could see the cars parked on the drive: her father's Mercedes next to Toby's Range Rover, and beside that the sleek sporting vehicle that Nick Destry must have arrived in. Dark, powerful and alien, she thought, like its owner. The unwanted intruder into the family circle.

Surely they couldn't have exhausted all other possibilities before turning to him.

The tap on the door made her jump. She stared across at the white-painted panels, her heart thumping idiotically, wishing they could be made transparent by some instant magic so that she could see who was waiting outside. Then she heard her father's voice call quietly, 'Paige—are you asleep?'

'No, Dad. Come in—please.' For a bemused second she didn't know whether to be relieved or sorry.

Francis Harrington's head appeared apologetically round the door. 'I don't want to disturb you, darling, especially if you're feeling unwell.'

She uncurled herself and stood up. 'I'm fine again, now. Really.' But it wasn't true, because she was shaking inside. Terrified to hear what he'd come to tell her. She braced herself. 'Did—did you want to talk?'

'I was hoping to have a word with you downstairs.' He hesitated, looking at her doubtfully. 'But it could always wait until morning.'

Paige pressed a switch and the wall lights sprang to life. She said, 'I think it had better be now. Don't you?'

'Perhaps.' He seated himself in the satin-covered easy chair and Paige resumed her place at the window, facing him, her hands gripping the edge of the cushion on either side of her.

There was a silence, then he said, 'Nick Destry, darling. What do you think of him?'

She swallowed, said carefully, 'I don't think of him at all. He's like all his kind—just a suit.'

He frowned. 'I'd say he's rather more than that.' He paused again. 'Do you positively dislike him? Please be frank with me.'

Frank? she asked herself. Good God, she couldn't even be honest with herself.

'Dad—I really don't know him well enough to make that kind of judgement. Why do you want to know? Is it important?'

He said heavily, 'Yes, my dear. In fact, the whole future of Harringtons depends on it.'

'On my opinion of Nick Destry.' Her laugh sounded forced—brittle. 'How—how is that possible?'

And she sat, her mind reeling into chaos, as he told her. As he spelled out the bargain that had been hammered out, and her role in it.

For a moment the world stopped. Nausea rose in her throat, and she wanted to scream *No* and go on screaming until they saw how impossible this thing was that they were asking of her.

She said, 'Is that why I was made to come here? So that he could look me over—see if I measure up to his stringent requirements?'

'Naturally, it was considered desirable that you should meet.'

'Desirable,' she repeated. 'Oh, yes. I—see that.'

She lifted her hands to her face. She remembered his eyes—the way they'd stripped the clothes from her body. The money held insolently in his fingers that evening in the wine bar. And—oh, God—just a few hours ago his touch.

Every instinct was urging her to refuse and let Harringtons work out its own salvation.

But she knew that she couldn't do that. Instead, she heard a stranger's voice speaking the words of agreement. Of compliance.

'Do we know when he'll want this non-marriage to take place?' she asked, cutting across Francis Harrington's stumbling words of thanks.

'As soon as the necessary arrangements can be made.

But it might be better if you were to discuss that with him yourself.'

'Must I?' Her throat tightened.

'Of course. And he'll wish to make you a formal proposal—to hear from you that you agree in principle...'

She said shortly, 'I don't think principles have much to do with this.'

He looked at her doubtfully. 'We're all eternally grateful to you, my dear. I want you to know that. And when we've surmounted our current problems perhaps we can find some way of easing Maitland Destry out of the picture altogether, so that you'll never have to see him again.'

Her smile was wintry. 'I don't plan to see that much of him anyway.'

'No,' he said. 'No, of course not. Well, I'll leave you now. Let you get some rest.'

Rest? Paige thought incredulously as the door closed behind him. She didn't feel as if she'd ever sleep again. There was only chaos and she was part of it.

What the hell had been going on at Harringtons? she asked herself. Was it Toby?

If she was honest, she'd always had doubts about his ability to run the company, but she'd stifled them. Told herself not to get involved. And this was the result. This hideous mess in which she was now involved up to her neck.

She wrapped her arms round the cold rigidity of her body and stood, teeth clenched to stop them chattering.

She thought, What have I done? Dear God, *what have I done?*

In spite of herself, she managed to doze fitfully for a few hours, but even during those brief periods she was pursued by strange disturbing dreams.

She awoke just after sunrise and lay staring at the stream of golden light pouring into the room. It was going to be a beautiful day, and there was a terrible irony in that somehow, because it was also going to be the worst day of her life. It ought to be marked by cold winds and sombre rain. Accompanied, if possible, by the kind of thunderstorm that got financiers struck by lightning.

She got up, because there seemed to be no point in staying in bed. No one else in the house would be stirring yet. It was far too early.

She showered, and dressed in a plain cotton shirt and a brief denim skirt, thrusting her bare feet into flat leather sandals.

She went noiselessly downstairs and made her way to the kitchen. She filled the kettle and put it on the range, then spooned coffee into a mug. Strong and black, she thought as she stirred the brew. Something to put heart in her.

She let herself quietly out of the back door and made her way round to the formal garden. There was something about the symmetrical beds and neat box hedges that she found calming to the spirit. It was where she did all her best thinking.

Except that today there was nothing to think about. Her decision had been made and there was no going back. Not if Harringtons was to survive and old Crispin's dream was going to be carried forward to the next generation.

Her great-grandfather had been very clear about what he expected. He wanted the best architects, the best materials and the top craftsmen to work on his developments. He wanted everything he built to be in harmony with its surroundings.

Yet now, in the twenty-first century, it seemed that for the first time his vision had faltered.

She walked slowly, sipping her scalding coffee, lifting her face to the sun. There'd been a heavy dew, and all the plants and leaves were glistening in the pure morning light.

Behind her, the house looked as if it had been rooted in the earth since the dawn of time.

Yet it had not always been so. Hampton Hall had been almost a ruin when Crispin Harrington had bought it, but he'd worked on it slowly, bringing it back to life and landscaping the neglected grounds like some eighteenth-century grandee.

He'd designed the formal garden, saved the old roses in the walled garden from extinction and added new ones, replanted all the lawns and cleared the lake, stocking it with carp.

A labour of love, she thought, and the results had silenced local critics who'd derisively nicknamed it 'Crispin's Folly' when the work had begun.

And it was that she was fighting for as much as the company. The Harrington heritage. And no one was going to take it away from them.

She walked across the damp grass to the edge of the lake and stood while she finished her coffee, watching the bubbles breaking the surface of the water as the fish rose.

She turned to go back to the house, then halted with a gasp, her heart hammering unevenly. Because she wasn't alone any more. The peace of the morning was already destroyed.

Because *he* was there. Standing at the head of the terrace steps, his dark figure looking as if it had been carved from obsidian. Standing between her and the house like the interloper he was.

She could hardly ignore him, and she certainly couldn't run, so she began slowly to walk back towards him. And saw him, equally unhurriedly, descend the steps and move towards her. Meeting her halfway, she thought shakily.

They halted a few yards from each other, like opponents in a duel. He was wearing black trousers that moulded his long legs and a matching cotton shirt, the cuffs rolled back to reveal tanned forearms. His eyes were narrowed and slightly wary.

He said unsmilingly, 'Good morning. I saw you from my window.'

'At this hour?' Paige mimicked astonishment, wondering if this meant he hadn't passed a particularly restful night either, and deriving a kind of jaundiced satisfaction from the possibility. She raised her eyebrows. 'Spying on me, Mr Destry?' she asked sweetly. 'Afraid I was going to throw myself into the lake and drown?'

'Neither.' She saw the firm mouth tighten. 'I merely thought this might be a convenient opportunity for us to talk.'

She said crisply, 'What is there to talk about? I'm sure my father told you last night that it's a done deal. That I've agreed to accept your—obscene proposition.'

There was a loaded silence, then he said, too gently, 'There's an easy way to do this, Miss Harrington, and a hard way. I suggest you choose your option carefully.' He paused. 'After all, I didn't formulate the rules of the Harrington board. Your great-grandfather was the one who left us both stranded between a rock and a hard place.'

She said stormily, 'Don't you dare say one word against Crispin. He had vision—and integrity. Something money-men like you can only aspire to.'

His mouth curled. 'And if old Crispin was standing here at this moment, Miss Harrington, how do you think he'd like the way his company has been run lately? I don't think "vision" or "integrity" are the words I'd pick.' He looked her over contemptuously. 'And let me remind you that without the intervention of this particular money man, these glorious surroundings you're enjoying would probably be going under the hammer.'

The sunny morning blurred suddenly, and Paige looked down at the flagged path, biting her lip hard.

She was aware of movement, his hand reaching out to her, and recoiled instinctively, terrified that he was going to touch her. Because the memory of what the mere brush of his fingers could do was all too potent. And if he touched her again, she thought wildly, she would burn. She might bleed. And the risk was just too great.

As their eyes met she saw his flare with astonishment and anger. Then he took a step back, thrusting his hands into his pockets with almost mocking emphasis.

He said, 'Feel safer now?'

Fighting to regain her self control, Paige did not answer.

After a moment, he said more quietly, 'I was only going to offer you a handkerchief. And an apology.' He threw his head back. 'I was too harsh just now, maybe, but I felt a note of realism was needed. The fact is no one's going to offer Harringtons the kind of investment it needs without strings. And I felt from the start that direct supervision was essential—which meant a seat on the board.' He shrugged. 'Unfortunately for us both, there was only one way to achieve that.'

She said, 'So it was your idea.'

'Yes, of course,' he said. 'But I won't apologise for that. Because if Harringtons is to survive there's really no alternative. Maitland Destry turned out to be the Last Chance Saloon.'

She winced. 'Thank you,' she said with irony, 'for making everything so clear.'

'Then let me clarify something else,' he came back at her. 'With a little mutual goodwill we can get through this without permanent damage. But we both have to work at it.'

'Yes,' she said. 'I—I can see that.' She hesitated. 'It's just that you're the last person in the world...' And faltered into silence under his sardonic glance.

He said levelly, 'Just try and remember it's not personal—it's strictly business.' His mouth twisted. 'To coin a phrase.'

'Yes.' Paige drew a deep breath. 'Well, if that's all you wanted to say, I'll get back to the house.'

He said slowly, 'I thought perhaps we could drop the confrontation—try to get to know each other a little.'

Paige shrugged. 'I don't see the need. As long as you recognise me at the ceremony itself, that's all that matters.'

Nick Destry sighed with exasperation. 'You really won't give an inch, will you, Miss Harrington? I understand how you must hate the feeling you've been—sold off, but...'

'But I'm not for sale, Mr Destry,' Paige said, swiftly and sharply. 'I'm strictly on loan. You get your seat on the board, and I get the quickest divorce in the history of the world.'

He said softly, 'Now that's what I call forward planning. Maybe you should be running Harringtons instead of your brother.'

She lifted her chin. 'I'm quite happy with the *status quo*, thanks.'

'Well, I'm not.' His smile did not reach his eyes. 'I foresee lively times ahead.'

She walked past him and went up the steps of the terrace, her skin tingling under the certainty that he was still watching her. Forbidding herself to look back to check.

A simple deal, she asked herself shakily. Somehow I don't think so. Dear God, what have I got myself into?

She went straight to her room, and remained there until she heard the breakfast gong. Toby waylaid her outside the dining room.

'Sis—I can't thank you enough...'

'Don't be too grateful.' Paige cut him short. 'I suspect we may have taken on more trouble than we ever dreamed of.'

He snorted. 'Destry's going to find he's a lone voice. Nothing's ever going to make him a Harrington, after all, and he's never been up against the whole family.' He smiled confidently. 'He can be sidelined.'

'Really?' Paige raised her eyebrows. 'You think Great-Uncle James or Cousin Roger and his nonentity of a wife are going to range themselves with you against the money? I wouldn't count on it.' She paused. 'In fact, I wouldn't count on anything.'

Nick was already at the table when she went in, eating bacon and scrambled eggs. He rose politely, holding the chair next to him for her, and with a murmured word of thanks she slid into it, aware of the searching glance he sent her.

'Well, you're a sly pair,' said Denise, busy pouring coffee. 'I really thought you'd only just met and Paige couldn't stand you.' She giggled, oblivious to Toby's furious glare. 'And it was only a lovers' tiff all along. Imagine.'

'Almost beyond belief,' Nick agreed gravely, his lower lip twitching very slightly.

Paige, shocked to find she wanted to laugh too, took a hasty sip of orange juice instead.

'I suppose the wedding will be in London,' Denise went on encouragingly, but Nick shook his head.

'I'm sure Paige will want to be married from her family home,' he said firmly. 'And at the village church. We'll arrange a time for next week with the vicar. Friday, perhaps.'

All eating stopped. Francis Harrington said, 'Isn't that something of a rush, my boy? A wedding takes a hell of a lot of organising.'

'Not with a special licence and no fuss.' Nick reached for the toast rack. 'Paige and I want a very quiet affair, don't we, darling? Now that I've finally got her to say yes, I really don't want to wait any longer.'

He smiled at her, and she tried and failed to make her facial muscles respond. She knew, too, that if she tried to say something only a strangled squeak would emerge.

'We thought—just immediate family,' Nick went on, buttering his toast. 'Apart from my best man, my only guest will be my grandmother.'

Denise's eyes were like saucers. 'Won't your parents be coming?'

'Unfortunately, no,' he said courteously. 'They both died a few years ago in one of those freak accidents only a few hundred yards away from home. A child ran into the road and my mother, who was driving, swerved to avoid him and hit a tree.'

'Oh, I'm so sorry.' Denise looked accusingly at her sister-in-law. 'Paige—you should have told us.'

Paige looked down at her plate. 'Yes,' she said woodenly. 'I'm—sorry.'

She meant it. There'd been a flatness in his voice as he'd told the story which suggested there was a residue of grief not yet dealt with. It made him seem suddenly uncomfortably human. And that wasn't what she wanted. Hatred needed feeding.

'Does your grandmother live in London?' Toby asked.

'Not any more. She's always hated cities, and when my grandfather died she moved back to the little village in Normandy where she was born.'

He took Paige's hand, and she had to fight with herself not to snatch it away. He said softly, 'She'll be delighted to hear our news, darling. She's always telling me that it's high time I settled down.'

'So you're part French,' Denise deduced brightly. 'How intriguing.'

'Oh, you don't know the half of it,' Paige told her with heavy irony, pushing away her untouched plate. 'He's just full of surprises.'

'If you've finished breakfast, darling, perhaps we could walk down to the village now,' Nick suggested, his fingers tightening in warning round hers. 'See if the vicar's at home and set the date.'

'Now just a minute—' Toby began, with a touch of aggression.

'Is there a problem?' Nick queried mildly, and Toby subsided.

'No,' he muttered. 'You—go ahead. I just don't want my sister to be rushed into anything—before she's ready. That's all.'

'I think you'll find she's just as eager as I am.' Nick slipped an arm round Paige's rigid waist. 'She's already making all kinds of plans for the future—aren't you, darling?'

Paige forced her lips into the semblance of a smile. 'I can hardly wait, sweetest.'

She walked beside him in silence down the lane leading to the village, between verges heavy with cow parsley. The sun was gloriously warm on her back and the air was alive with the hum of bees and the distant growl of a tractor. It was an idyllic pastoral scene, yet Paige might as well have been walking into purgatory.

'A perfect day,' Nick commented at last.

'We clearly have very different ideas on perfection,' she said curtly.

'Probably,' he returned with equal sharpness. 'But it would be good if we could bury our differences until after the wedding. Or this cover story of a whirlwind romance isn't going to fool anyone.'

She bit her lip. 'Is that what we're telling people?' Her voice was scornful. 'That it was love at first sight?'

He shrugged. 'Why not? It happens.' He paused. 'And it's better than the truth in this situation.'

'I don't see why,' Paige objected.

'Think.' His tone bit. 'The financial press will be featuring the fact that I've joined the Harrington board. That's unavoidable. But any hint that it's been done by way of an arranged marriage will have the tabloids crawling all over us. And none of us want that—personally or professionally.'

'No,' she allowed unwillingly. 'But do you think we'll really fool anyone?'

'Not a soul,' he said, 'while you maintain your present attitude. And your brother doesn't help either,' he added with a touch of grimness. 'Maybe you could remind him it's a bit late to play the protective card where you're concerned.'

'Very well,' she said. 'In return, perhaps you could cut back on the endearments.'

'They're built into the script, I'm afraid,' he said. 'And people not in on our guilty secret, like your sister-in-law, will expect something of the kind.'

'I—suppose so.' Paige shook her head despairingly. 'Oh, God, it all gets worse and worse.'

He halted. Before she could take evasive action his hands gripped her shoulders, turning her to face him. The dark eyes were hard as they surveyed her flushed face.

'It's not too late,' he told her harshly. 'You don't have to be a martyr to the Harrington cause if it's really so repellent. You can still pull out.'

'What about you?' She wrenched herself free. 'You could forego your seat on the board and still lend Harringtons the money.'

'And give Brother Toby a blank cheque?' he asked coldly. 'Not a chance, sweetheart. I prefer to see where my money's going.'

She stared at the ground. 'I've given my word,' she said

at last. 'I can't back out. However much I might want to,' she added defiantly.

'A virgin sacrifice on the family altar,' Nick said mockingly. 'How incredibly noble. Or, should I say, amazingly venal.'

Paige gasped. She said chokingly, 'You say that—you *dare* to say that to me?'

Her hand swung back to slap the derision from his face, but he forestalled her, his fingers closing implacably round her wrist, jerking her towards him.

For a moment she swayed, off-balance, and felt his arms close round her without gentleness. Felt the hardness of his body against hers.

He said, 'You once offered me ten pounds for a kiss, darling. Well, have this one for free.'

Frightened, Paige put her hands against his chest in an attempt to push him away, but it was too late for that. The next second his mouth had taken hers. The kiss was unhurried, even calculating, but there was anger there, and insolence too.

It was being inflicted as punishment, and she knew it, but that made it no easier to endure, held helpless in the circle of his arms.

She made a small sound of protest in her throat and tried desperately to turn away. Begging wordlessly for her release.

Instead, Nick's hand came up to cradle her head, and she felt his fingers twist in the silky strands of her hair, holding her still while his lips parted hers, so that he could invade the heated sweetness of her mouth with his tongue.

Suddenly she was swamped by a strange and dizzying intensity, carried away to a new and undreamed of dimension by the deepening intimacy of the kiss.

His mouth scorched like the sun. The fragrance of earth, grass and leaves seemed echoed in the scent of his skin.

His body was quickening, unequivocally urgent against hers.

She was captive, in subjection to some deep primeval force she had never experienced before.

She was beyond reason or understanding, because behind her closed lids the world was spinning out of control. She was giddy—shaking—hardly able to breathe—her legs turning to water. Oblivious to everything but the dazed clamour of her senses.

And then, with the shock of a blow, it was over and she was free. Her eyes opened in bewilderment to find he'd stepped back, putting several feet of sunlit country road between them. She stared at him, struggling to think coherently, her hand going up instinctively to touch the newly swollen contours of her mouth.

'Well, well,' Nick said softly, eyes narrowed. 'There's never a convenient haystack when you want one.' And he began to laugh.

It was like being doused with icy water.

Her voice shook, 'You utter bastard. You imagine for one minute that I'd…that I'd let you…?'

'Unfortunately, we'll never know.' He shrugged. 'But at least you look more of a bride-to-be and less of a martyr, which should convince the vicar of our sincerity. Shall we go?'

She wanted to damn his eyes. To shriek that she wouldn't walk as far as the next gateway with him.

Instead she heard herself saying hoarsely, 'I want you to promise—to swear—that you'll leave me alone from now on.'

'Fine,' he said equably. And paused. 'If that's what you want.'

'Yes,' she said fiercely. 'Yes—it is.'

'Although I suspect,' he went on as if she hadn't spoken,

'that you don't even know what you want. Not any more. But that, my future wife, is your problem, not mine.'

And he turned away, walking towards the village, leaving her, reluctantly, to follow.

If she'd been hoping the vicar would declare the parish church booked for months and their marriage an impossibility, she was to be disappointed.

Reverend Winship, a quiet silver-haired man, was clearly surprised, but agreed that the ceremony could take place as soon as the special licence had been obtained.

'Although I'm old-fashioned enough to prefer the banns to be called,' he added wistfully. 'I suppose you wouldn't consider…?'

'We'd prefer not to wait,' Nick cut in swiftly. 'Would we, darling?'

Paige stared down at the pattern on the carpet. 'No,' she said bleakly. 'The sooner the better.'

'Ah,' Reverend Winship said tactfully, and left it at that.

'My God,' Paige said, appalled, when they got outside. 'He must think I'm pregnant.'

'Then he'll know he's wrong when we don't book a christening,' Nick returned indifferently.

'But he's known me all my life.' She was suddenly absurdly close to tears. 'I hate deceiving him—having him think badly of me. I'm going to feel such a hypocrite—standing in front of him pretending that I want to be married, when all the time…'

There was a silence, then he said quietly, 'Let's accept that it's not what either of us would have chosen and leave it at that.'

'Oh, that's easy for you to say,' she said savagely. 'It's not your life—or your reputation—in ruins.'

His mouth tightened. 'You really think you're the only one making a sacrifice, don't you, lady? Well, take it from me, this bargain of ours is a two-edged sword. I also have a life.'

'Well, please don't change it on my account.' Her tone was taut. 'After all, we're going to need grounds for the ultimate divorce.'

'You mean you're giving me permission to commit adultery?' Nick jeered. 'What would the vicar say if he could hear you now? In any case, forget it,' he added harshly. 'The terms are strictly two years' separation. Neat, tidy and without scandal.'

'I hope,' she said icily, 'that you're proud of your deal.'

'Wait until I've brought Harringtons back from the brink,' he returned with equal coldness. 'Then ask me again.'

He paused. 'Perhaps you'd forgive me if I don't escort you back to the Hall. I think both of us would prefer to be alone.'

'Yes,' she said. 'Perhaps that would be—best.'

She stood, watching the tall figure stride away from her, around the corner by the church, where he was lost to view.

Out of sight, Paige thought. But not, unfortunately, out of mind.

Somehow she was going to have to find a cure for that. And it would need to be a permanent one—that was if she was ever to have any peace of mind again.

And slowly she began the long walk home.

CHAPTER FIVE

'PAIGE. *Paige.*' Nick's impatient voice invaded her reverie and brought the real world stinging suddenly into focus. 'Are you listening?'

She found herself blinking dazedly as she encountered the questioning look he was directing at her over the back of his seat.

'I'm sorry. I—I was miles away.'

'Wishful thinking, I fear.' The firm mouth curled. 'This is very definitely the here and now, and the message from Hilaire is to tighten our seatbelts. We're in for the proverbial bumpy ride.'

'Oh.' One apprehensive glance out of the window showed her that the sea below them was no longer still and flat. The high slate-coloured waves were crested with angry white foam. The sky was a dark blanket and the horizon invisible.

She bit her lip. 'It looks as if the storm has caught up with us.'

'It's moved up a notch,' Nick said drily. 'It's now officially a Hurricane. They've christened it Minna.'

'Oh, God.' She stiffened in dismay, her fingers clamped to the arms of her seat.

'But Hilaire says this is only the edge of it,' he went on briskly, 'and that we'll soon be at Sainte Marie. Just as planned.'

'Yes,' Paige said, touching the tip of her tongue to her dry lips as the plane lurched suddenly. 'Yes, of course.'

Nick's gaze sharpened. 'Nervous?' he asked, the tiny mannerism not lost on him.

'Not at all,' she denied swiftly. 'Just a little thirsty, that's all.'

'You'll find some drinks in the cold bag under your seat. And don't worry,' he added, more gently. 'Hilaire knows what he's doing.'

'Yes,' she said again. And, 'Thank you.'

She uncapped some still mineral water, repressing an instinctive cry of alarm as the plane juddered again.

'Are you sure you're all right?' He was still watching her, damn him.

'Perfectly.' She drank some more water. 'Please don't fuss. It's only a bit of turbulence, after all,' she added with an assumption of nonchalance.

Besides, nothing the hurricane threw at her could compare with the emotional storm now churning inside her, she thought wretchedly.

It was incredible how vivid her recollection had been. It seemed that she was cursed with total recall over every painful moment she'd spent with Nick. The passage of time hadn't blurred a thing.

She'd almost felt the sun-warmed stones of the church-yard wall under her hand as she'd stood watching Nick's departure.

But then Nick walking away would always be one of her most potent memories, she told herself, her fingers tightening almost convulsively on the arms of her seat. Because it had happened so often during the brief entanglement of their lives.

It was encountering him again so unexpectedly that had prompted all this inner turmoil, she thought. Usually she had the past well under control. But now events were conspiring against her to stir the memory banks into action again.

Another gust caught the plane and she closed her eyes, making herself breathe deeply and evenly, aware that the churning inside her had become swiftly and unpleasantly physical with the increase in turbulence.

You are never air-sick, she told herself with grim determination. And, anyway, you cannot be ill in front of *him.* That would be a disaster.

Nor can you let him see that you're terrified in case, for all Hilaire's experience, that hostile stretch of ocean down there might be waiting to swallow you up.

Sips of water helped her resolve as the aircraft battered its way to Sainte Marie with what seemed agonising slowness. But she was dizzy with fighting her nausea, and shaking like a leaf by the time Hilaire coaxed the plane skilfully down on to the runway.

'Safe and sound,' Nick commented as he fastened his briefcase. 'And ahead of schedule too.'

Well, she had that to be thankful for at least, Paige thought, forcing her trembling limbs to obey her. She hadn't missed her onward flight, as she'd feared, and soon—very soon now—she'd be back in England—and safety.

Except—how safe was safe? she wondered restlessly as she gathered her belongings. What were the problems Nick had hinted at on the beach the previous night? She'd planned to ring home after breakfast and have a word with Toby, so that she could see exactly what she might have to deal with, but the advent of Hurricane Minna had distracted her.

Now she hung back deliberately, to allow Nick to reach the terminal building before she did and—hopefully—be lost in the crowd. The shrieking wind savaged her all the way across the tarmac, and she was breathless and almost deafened by the time she got to the main hall.

Not unexpectedly, it was crowded with agitated people—some of them milling about aimlessly, others seated on their stacked luggage.

Paige realised, heart sinking, that none of the check-ins seemed to be operating, and joined the queue for the enquiry desk.

When she reached it, her worst fears were confirmed.

'I'm sorry, *m'dame*.' The clerk was polite, but definite. 'All flights are grounded.'

'Until when?'

He shrugged. 'Until further notice—and certainly until Hurricane Minna has finished with us.'

'But what am I going to do?' Paige asked, dismayed, glancing around her. 'Can I stay here?'

He shook his head. 'We will shortly be closing the airport.' He took another look at her proffered ticket and frowned, his attention sharpening. 'Just a minute, *m'dame*. I believe there is a message for you.' He glanced down a sheet of paper lying beside him. 'Yes, Miss Harrington, there is a car waiting to take you to the Hotel Marie Royale, where a room has been reserved on your behalf.'

'A room?' Paige echoed in bewilderment. 'I don't understand. I've made no booking.'

'Nevertheless it exists, *m'dame*.' He handed back her ticket. 'I advise you to make use of your car quickly. There will not be many more trips,' he added warningly, 'and it is a long walk into town.'

The driver was waiting impatiently, and grumbled under his breath throughout the journey.

The road into town was already littered with debris, Paige saw, and the palm trees which lined it were bending double under the force of the gale.

When they reached the hotel he almost snatched the money from her hand and drove off with a squeal of tyres. Not that she could blame him, Paige acknowledged wryly as she battled her way into the hotel.

The foyer was packed, and the queues for the reception desk seemed endless. Paige had plenty of time to look warily about her, but thankfully Nick was nowhere to be seen—yet again.

He's probably already on his way home, she thought. Walking on the water.

She still couldn't believe there was a room for her here. Ahead of her, people were being politely but firmly turned away and retreating, their faces resigned or disappointed.

'A mattress in the dining room,' one woman sighed to her husband. 'I suppose it's better than nothing.'

When Paige reached the desk, she said, 'I believe you have a room for me. Paige Harrington.'

She was fully expecting to be laughed at, or offered another mattress, but instead the desk clerk shot her a quick glance, then turned to his computer screen.

'Yes, *madame.*' He signalled to a bellboy. 'Take this lady's bag to Room 105.'

Paige was aware of discontented mutters behind her, and a voice saying loudly, 'All right for some.'

She said, 'I don't understand. I didn't make any reservation.'

'We received a telephone call from St Antoine first thing this morning, *madame.*' He handed her the key, then looked past her to the next hopeful. 'That's how we were able to accommodate you.'

Brad, Paige thought, numb with gratitude as she followed the bellboy to the lift. He must have guessed she'd probably be stuck here, and had acted to make sure she had somewhere to sleep.

Without doubt he was one special man, she acknowledged with a sigh. And she wished with all her heart she could return his regard in the way he wanted.

The room was in total darkness, and for a moment she hesitated on the threshold. Then the bellboy flicked the light switch, and Paige realised that the reason for the gloom was the substantial shutters that had been placed over the windows.

Obviously the Marie Royale was accustomed to the possibility of severe weather, and well prepared for it.

But it was a beautiful room—the walls painted a cool, pale blue and the wide bed made up with immaculate white linen.

The boy put her bag on the rack provided, showed her the bathroom and the closets, and told her that, although the dining room was being used as a dormitory, a cold buffet would be served throughout the day in the ballroom. He then departed cheerfully, clutching his tip.

When he'd gone Paige switched off the main light, leaving one of the shaded lamps on the night tables which flanked the bed as the room's sole illumination.

She sank down on the edge of the bed, easing off her sandals with a sigh. She knew she ought to take off her linen trouser suit and hang it up before it became creased to the point of extinction, but she didn't have the energy. Her stomach hadn't yet settled after that nightmare flight, and her whole body felt clammy with perspiration.

The cold buffet held not the slightest attraction for her, she decided. In fact, given the choice, she would probably never eat again. Nor did she fancy leaving the privacy and comparative peace of this room and joining the crowd downstairs, who were likely to become increasingly fractious and wound up as the weather deteriorated.

She, of course, was so calm and together, she derided herself.

But it wasn't just the trip that had upset her, she thought, lifting her legs on to the bed and settling herself back against the softness of the pillows with a sigh. Or the prospect of being trapped here while the hurricane blew itself out.

Even if the flight had been as smooth as silk, Nick's

presence on the aircraft would have provided sufficient disturbance all by itself.

All these months she'd managed to avoid him, physically if not mentally, she thought unhappily, cursing the coincidence which had thrown them together at such a time.

She closed her eyes. Lack of sleep the previous night was getting to her as well. Maybe a nap would help calm her down.

A gust of wind rattled the shutters and made her shiver, burrow more deeply into the mattress. If this was just the edge of the storm, she thought, then what the hell would it be like to be caught in the middle?

Although she should know, because it was a situation that seemed to have been pursuing her all her life. Finding herself stuck, as she was now, between the devil and the deep sea.

The devil, of course, being Nick, and Harrington Holdings the bottomless ocean.

Looking back, she saw that in the rush of preparations for her hasty wedding she'd hardly had time to think, or question what she was doing. But the sense of relief emanating from Toby and her father had been almost tangible, so she'd supposed it had to be the right thing.

And, family loyalty notwithstanding, maybe the company had needed an outside eye, dispassionate and even clinical, to put it back on the right path again.

Thankfully there had been neither the time nor the need for the usual wedding trappings—although the housekeeper had insisted on making a cake and persuaded a friend, who was an expert in sugarcraft at the local Womens' Institute, to ice it for her.

Nothing would have induced Paige to wear white, so she'd hunted in the local boutiques until she'd found a plain shift dress, beautifully cut in heavy primrose silk and topped by a gauzy jacket striped in primrose, cream and silver that floated round her like mist. Even Denise had admitted grudgingly that it was quite pretty.

A few days before the wedding a girl introducing herself as Gina Norton, Nick's personal assistant, had rung to ask if her passport was in order.

'Yes, of course.' Paige had frowned. 'Why do you need to know?'

The other girl gave an engaging gurgle of laughter. 'Nick asked me to check, Miss Harrington. I guess he's taking you abroad for your honeymoon.'

'Honeymoon?' Paige echoed dazedly. 'You surely don't mean that?' She checked, aware that she was on dangerous ground.

'It is usual, Miss Harrington.' Gina Norton sounded bewildered now, and Paige hurriedly pulled herself together.

'I didn't think there'd be time to organise anything,' she offered lamely. 'I know how busy Nick must be.'

'Oh, he'll make time for this, all right,' Gina said cheerfully. 'What man wouldn't?'

Paige bit her lip. 'I suppose so.' She paused. 'Have you any idea where he's planning to go?'

'I'm afraid not,' Gina apologised. 'I think he wants to surprise you.'

Then he's succeeded, Paige thought grimly as she replaced her receiver. It was only part of the general charade, of course, but there was such a thing as carrying pretence too far, and she couldn't pretend that the brief exchange had not unsettled her.

On the day of the wedding itself Paige was aware of a curious sense of total unreality. If the church had been full, she thought detachedly as the organist struck up the 'Wedding March', and she began the long progress up the aisle on her father's arm, she doubted whether she could have gone through with it. But fortunately she only had a handful of people to face.

And one of them, of course, was Nick.

She saw him move out of the front pew to wait for her at the chancel steps, tall and lean in yet another of his elegant dark suits. And for a moment time rushed back, and she found herself remembering in dizzying detail those few moments she had spent in his arms. She experienced again the pressure of his mouth on hers, the hot, musky invasion of his tongue, and the uncompromising strength of his body against hers.

And, most telling of all, the sudden shamed excess of her own arousal.

For a moment she faltered, aware, as she did so, of her father's concerned sideways glance. As she struggled to regain her equilibrium she realised that Nick was watching too, his gaze fixed on every step she took towards him, his eyes hooded and impenetrable. As if he was mesmerising her, she thought, her throat tightening. Controlling her movements. Making sure she didn't turn and run.

But the time for that was long past. She was committed now, and she would go through with her unpalatable role, whatever the cost.

She reached his side and handed Denise the flowers that had arrived for her that morning with Nick's card—yellow freesias and tiny cream roses bound with silver ribbons.

'He rang to ask about colours,' her sister-in-law had confided smugly.

But not, Paige thought, to speak to herself. She hadn't received a letter or a personal telephone call from him since the day they'd parted in the village. Even the passport enquiry had been dealt with by an underling.

In fact, she'd wondered more than once if he might be the one to back away when the chips were down.

Yet here he was, a silent presence beside her as Reverend Winship spoke the familiar, dignified words from the *Book of Common Prayer*.

We should have gone to a registry office, Paige thought guiltily. These vows are too solemn, too meaningful for what we're doing. So why did Nick insist?

His hand was strong and cool as it took hers. The ring he'd chosen was gold and completely plain. It felt heavy and alien on her finger and she stared down at it, wondering if she would have time to become accustomed to it before the marriage ended.

She was thankful that Reverend Winship was an old-fashioned man, and that, accordingly, there were no jocular exhortations to Nick to 'kiss the bride.'

As they walked back down the aisle together Paige was aware of the critical gaze of an upright elderly lady sitting in the second pew. She was wearing a grey silk suit, and a sweep of black straw crowned her upswept white hair. As Paige drew level with her she bowed slightly, but did not smile.

That must be Nick's grandmother, Paige thought, feeling slightly chilled. Someone else we have to deceive—and something tells me that it might not be so easy…

In the car, she found herself huddling into her corner, her fingers nervously playing with the ribbons on her bouquet.

'Relax,' Nick advised sardonically. He nodded towards the driver behind his glass partition. 'I never pounce in front of an audience.'

'That's reassuring.' She pulled at the petals of an inoffensive freesia. 'But there won't always be one.'

'True,' he said softly. 'So you'll just have to trust me.'

'Not easy.' Paige drew a deep breath. 'When you spring unpleasant surprises like honeymoons on me.'

He lifted an indifferent shoulder. 'It's what newly married couples do, my sweet.' He paused. 'Anyway, I thought you could probably do with a few days' break.'

'Perhaps,' she said. 'But not with you.'

'I come with the territory, I'm afraid.' He didn't sound even remotely regretful. 'We do nothing that might alert people to the fact that this is not a conventional marriage. That was the deal, and I'm holding you to it.'

'You can't make me go with you.' Paige lifted her chin defiantly.

Nick sighed. 'Let's not start by arguing about what I can or cannot do. As things stand, I imagine your family would prefer you to be amenable.'

'I've been amenable,' she said. She lifted the hand with his ring on it. 'And there's the proof. But having you control my life is something else.'

'What the hell did you think was going to happen?' Nick demanded coldly. 'That I'd simply wave you farewell at the church door? Get real, lady.'

'But it's not real.' Paige brushed the fallen freesia petals from her dress with an impatient gesture. 'None of it. And I'm not sure I can handle it.'

'Then the next few days will give you plenty of opportunity to practise,' Nick drawled. 'When we come back you should be word-perfect. You can even start dropping hints that the honeymoon was less than blissful, if that will satisfy your thirst for truth,' he added curtly. 'Start preparing your acquaintances for the ultimate divorce. After all, we wouldn't be the first couple to marry in haste and repent with equal speed.'

'Yes, I suppose—' She broke off, staring unseeingly at the fleeing countryside. 'It's just not the way I ever visualised beginning married life.'

'Well, don't take it to heart,' Nick said as the car slowed for the turn into the Hall's driveway. 'Just think how much better it will be next time.'

'First,' she said, 'I have to learn to survive this.' She paused. 'I presume your grandmother doesn't know the truth. What on earth did you tell her?'

His smile was tight-lipped. 'Why, that it was love at first sight, darling—what else? And that we couldn't bear to wait for each other a second longer than we had to.'

'And she believed that?'

Nick shrugged. 'Who knows. Grandmère generally keeps her own counsel. Whatever, she's offered us her house for the honeymoon. She's going to stay in London and look up some old friends.'

'Oh,' Paige said numbly. If she had to spend some time in Nick's company, she would prefer to do so in the impersonality of a hotel, she thought. It seemed almost treacherous to take advantage of his grandmother's hospitality.

'Don't worry,' Nick said softly as the car drew up at the front door and Mrs Nixon emerged smilingly to welcome them. 'It's a big house. With care, we might be able to avoid each other the whole time we're there.'

'It's never too soon to begin,' Paige said—and, head held high, she walked into the house.

They did not have time to linger at the reception. Toasts were drunk to them, to which Nick responded briefly and wittily, and the cake was cut. Then Paige found herself upstairs, trying to decide what to pack for a week in Normandy before they left to catch a plane to Dinard.

She'd had a short, rather stilted conversation with Madame de Charrier, to whom she'd been formally presented by Nick. He was clearly very fond of his grandmother, but also slightly in awe of her, which Paige found interesting. A hint of weakness, she thought.

Casting round for something to say, she'd thanked the older woman for the loan of her house.

'I hope we haven't driven you away,' she'd added politely.

'No, I spend time in London each year. I like to visit the theatre and shop.' She had paused, her eyes fixed on Paige in shrewd assessment. 'And I have you to thank also, *mon enfant.*'

'I don't understand.'

'It is simple. For years I have been telling my grandson that it was time that he married, settled down, but always he made some excuse. Yet all it needed, it seems, was for him to see the woman of his dreams and *voilà,* the deed was done. And so fast, too. I did not know he was capable of such ardour.' She had smiled thinly. 'My felicitations.'

Paige could only hope that *madame* had attributed the heightened colour in her face to bridal shyness rather than guilt.

She threw mainly casual wear into her case—shorts, cotton trousers and tops, with a couple of informal dresses for evening. *Madame* had told her the house was not far from the sea, so she added a swimsuit, and some comfortable flat-heeled sandals so that she could explore the surrounding countryside on foot. Any excuse to get away from the house, she thought, her mouth twisting ruefully.

Because, in spite of all his guarantees, there was no escaping the fact that she was about to spend a week with a man who was still a totally unknown quantity. And to remind herself that it was just the same for him was no comfort at all.

She wasn't sure it was even true. Nick had seemed from the first to be able to predict her reactions and responses with infuriating accuracy. She felt she was being wrong-footed all the time, which did not make him easy company.

But—what the hell? The only company she should really be concerned about was Harringtons. That was why she was involved in this mess—to safeguard its future. And surely that was worth the sacrifice. Wasn't it?

Biting her lip, she returned to her unwanted task.

If she'd been packing for a real honeymoon all kinds of

filmy trifles would have gone into her luggage, with something white and decorously enticing for the coming night.

As it was, her choice of lingerie was strictly working-girl. Practical, she thought judiciously, and pretty too—but without a trace of seduction. Which was probably just as well under the circumstances.

Not that Nick would even see it, she made haste to remind herself. As he'd said, it was a big house, and she would choose a room as far from his as it was possible to get without actually burrowing into the walls.

She changed into a simple shirtwaister in blue chambray, and brushed her hair loose from its wedding style. A glance in the mirror told her that she looked much the same as always. Only the ring on her finger was there to remind her that her life had changed.

But not for long, she told herself with determination. And crossed her fingers too—just to be on the safe side.

Lying in the semi-darkness, listening to the howl of the wind, Paige found herself repeating the same superstitious gesture. Soon   soon the storm would blow away, and she'd be able to get back to England and sanity. That was what she had to keep telling herself. The kind of reassurance she so desperately needed.

Once she was home she would begin to see things rationally, in proportion again. And with every day that passed her freedom would draw a step nearer too.

Also, Nick would be so much easier to avoid on UK soil. After all, she'd turned keeping out of his way into a fine art over the past months. Now she had to dodge him mentally too.

So, she'd do what she always did. She'd stop thinking about him. Quite calmly and deliberately put him out of her mind. Close the door on the memories and turn the key.

It was her way of coping with what had happened between them, and so far it had worked perfectly. And she would make it work again—now. All it needed was a little will-power.

She closed her eyes and let her mind drift back over the last few days and weeks, thinking of Jack and Angela, and their happiness. The aura of completeness that seemed to surround them. Which was only how it should be, of course.

How, indeed, she'd assumed it would be for her—when the time came. When there was someone in her life.

She hadn't allowed for the demands of expediency, as it forced its way into her life and took over...

She checked herself right there. Because that was a road she should not go down.

Think back, she told herself, to a time when you were genuinely happy. Focus on that instead.

But the ritual didn't work its usual magic. There were too many other things interrupting—getting in the way. And her mind was tired, anyway, running in circles. Touching the edges of memory without settling.

Rest, she thought. Oh, God, I need to rest.

But how could she sleep with this wind shrieking, battering itself against the shutters, against the entire fabric of the building?

She thought, It can never happen. And slept.

She awoke slowly and unwillingly, and lay for a moment, wondering what had disturbed her after only—what? She looked at her watch. A couple of hours.

But a new note, it seemed, had entered the hurricane's relentless threnody. It was raining hard, the insistent splash of water sounding so loud that it might almost have been coming from inside the room.

She glanced upwards, half expecting to see that the rain had penetrated the roof and was falling through the ceiling to the tiled floor beside the bed. But there was no ominous brown stain visible on the white plaster, and the floor was dry too.

Yet the sound of running water was louder than ever, Paige thought, propping herself, puzzled, on to an elbow. She looked across the room and saw that the bathroom door was standing ajar, and the light was on.

Odd, because she could have sworn that she'd closed it—and switched off the light.

Oh, what does that matter? she thought in impatient dismissal. I hardly knew what I was doing earlier. And the fact is that's where the flood's coming from. So I'll have to investigate—see what the damage is. Although I don't suppose there'll be much they can do about it until the storm's passed over.

She swung herself off the bed and trod barefoot to the bathroom door, pushing it wider and taking a cautious step inside.

As she did so the rush of water stopped. The door of the shower cubicle opened and Nick stepped out, dark hair slicked to his head, moisture gleaming on every inch of naked skin as he reached for a towel.

Paige heard herself cry out, a small hoarse sound that she tried vainly to smother with her shaking hands.

He paused for a moment, brows lifting as he assimilated her presence, then he took the top towel from the stack—but not to cover himself, as she'd expected. Instead he began to dry himself, as if he was still alone.

She said in a voice she barely recognised. 'How did you get in here? And what the hell do you think you're doing?'

His tone was cool, clipped. 'I used my key, and I should have thought it was obvious what I was doing.' He paused, then added more gently, 'However, I didn't mean to wake you, and I'm sorry. I wanted to grab a shower before the water goes off.'

'A key?' Paige repeated. 'You have a key—to this room?'

'Of course,' he said. 'That's how the system operates. You rent a room. They give you a key.' He wound the damp towel round his hips and knotted it in place, taking another towel to dry his hair.

'But this is my room,' she said huskily. 'Rented for me by—someone.'

Nick shook his head. 'Wrong, my sweet. This is our room—rented for us by me.' He threw her a mocking smile. 'I was hoping you'd congratulate me on my foresight. It was the last one they had.'

'*You* did it?' She'd been so sure it was Brad. So grateful. And now—this living nightmare.

'Then you can have it all to yourself.' She backed into the bedroom, almost stumbling in her haste. 'I'll take my chances downstairs.'

'I don't advise it.' He'd followed her and was leaning against the doorframe—hideously at ease, she noticed furiously, and that bloody towel barely adequate for the task. 'Some of the local lowlife has arrived, and things could get ugly.'

'Compared to remaining here,' Paige said icily, 'it sounds almost appealing.'

Nick grinned. 'I guess that's my cue to bow my head in shame and leave you in possession of the field, or, in this case, the bed. Only it's not going to happen, darling. I'm staying right here. And so, incidentally, are you. Or I might be forced to fetch you back. And I'm sure you wouldn't like that.' He paused. 'Do I make myself clear, my sweet wife?'

The silence between them seemed endless—stretched out to screaming point and beyond.

Then, from some far distance, Paige heard herself say, 'Yes.'

CHAPTER SIX

'A WISE decision,' Nick applauded lazily.

Paige bit her lip hard. Everything about him was a torment, she thought stormily, from that faintly husky drawl to the expensively tanned skin he displayed without a hint of self-consciousness. Nature seemed to have designed him specially to set her nerve-endings jangling.

She said stonily, 'I have yet to be convinced of that. In the meantime, maybe you'd do me the courtesy of putting on some clothes.'

His brows lifted mockingly. 'Turned prude, darling? After all, you've seen me stripped before. Or had you forgotten?'

No she wanted to scream at him. I've forgotten nothing about that night. Every detail's right there in my memory as if it had been branded there.

Instead she shrugged. 'Not,' she said, 'a recollection I cherish.'

'I'm sorry,' he said. 'I shall try to avoid offending your susceptibilities during the remainder of our time together.' He looked her over. 'You, on the other hand, appear to be overdressed.'

'Not to my own taste,' Paige said, silently thanking her stars that she hadn't removed her ill-used trouser suit after all.

'Just as you wish,' Nick said courteously. 'But I suspect you're going to be very hot and even more crumpled by the time we get out of here, so I suggest you relax and change into something cooler for the sake of your own well-being.' He paused. 'Particularly relax.'

'This is hardly a restful situation.'

'It can be whatever we make it,' Nick returned. 'But maintaining your current attitude won't help.'

'*My* attitude?' Paige heard her voice rise. 'My God, you barge in here while I'm asleep, wander around with no clothes on, and I'm supposed to just *accept* it?'

The dark eyes narrowed in amusement. He said softly, 'I'd prefer you to welcome or even enjoy it, but I'll settle for acceptance if that's as good as it gets.' He paused. 'In deference to your wishes, I'll dress, and then the bathroom's all yours. I recommend you use the shower sooner rather than later, in case the water supply does go off. I gather it's possible.'

'Thank you,' she said. 'You're just a goldmine of good advice today.'

'Whereas you, darling, are a very different kind of mine—just waiting to explode.' His mouth twisted. 'Take a shower, Paige. It might calm you down. Unravel the kinks. Because in the present climate this room seems to be shrinking by the second, and we may be here for some time.'

She couldn't argue about that. The wind was screaming round the building, tearing at its structure, making it creak and groan. She could hear, in the distance, interior doors banging, adding to the incessant rattle of the heavy window shutters, and it scared her.

She'd never liked extremes—in human behaviour as well as weather, she thought ruefully. She was strictly a middle-of-the-road girl. She liked to be in control of her environment and feelings, and now everything seemed to be spiralling dangerously away from her, and there wasn't a damned thing she could do about it.

She lifted her chin. 'Are you suggesting a temporary truce?'

'If that's the best you have to offer,' he said. Once again

she was aware of the drift of his eyes over her rigid body. 'But you and I are going to have a serious talk at some point.'

Some inner alarm sounded, and she moved sharply in negation. 'We both have firms of expensive lawyers to do that for us.'

'But I prefer the direct approach.' His tone was clipped. 'So you're going to have to steel yourself, my love.'

'Oblige me by cutting out the endearments,' Paige said curtly. 'That is, if you want this truce to work.'

'Oh, I do,' Nick said softly. 'And it's in your own best interests too, believe me.'

He lounged across to his open suitcase, standing on the rack in the corner, and extracted briefs, pale blue cotton trousers and a white shirt.

'I hope these are enough to spare your blushes,' he murmured as he went back to the bathroom, the glance he cast her holding a faint glint of derision.

She made no answer. As the bathroom door closed behind him she sank down on the edge of the bed, her hands convulsively gripping the covers in a vain effort to stop them shaking.

This was a nightmare, she thought, and she didn't even have the comfort of knowing that she would soon wake from it.

She couldn't even feel grateful that he'd provided her with a comfortable shelter from the storm, because experience warned her that he wasn't doing it from the goodness of his heart. And she didn't even want to guess at his real motives.

She felt as if a trap had been set for her, and she'd walked right into it.

I should have known, she thought bitterly. From the moment I saw him at the Waterfront Club I should have realised that I wasn't going to walk away unscathed.

We were a collision waiting to happen, and if it hadn't been Hurricane Minna it would have been something else. As it is, this damned storm has just played into his hands. Like everything else in his charmed life.

A sharp rap at the bedroom door brought her to her feet. Maybe it was someone come to tell her it was all a mistake, and that there was another room for her elsewhere.

But when she answered the knock she found only a nervous-looking waiter with a room service trolley which he pushed into the room.

'Miz Destry?' He held out a bill pad. 'Sign, please.'

For a moment she stared at him, bewildered by his use of her married name. 'I didn't order anything…'

'No, ma'am. Your husband did that.'

Your husband. I could do without the constant reminders, Paige thought as she signed the account. She reached for her bag to give the waiter a tip, but he was already scuttling to the door and gone.

Paige began to lift the lids on the various dishes. Chicken sandwiches, she saw, and shrimp in a rice salad, and tiny savoury flans that she knew from experience were hotly flavoured with chilli.

In addition there was a platter of sliced pineapple, a tall insulated pot of coffee and, for no good reason that she could imagine, champagne on ice. And beside the champagne, incongruously, a handful of candles and a box of matches.

'Ah, the food.' Nick strolled out of the bathroom, pushing damp dark hair back from his forehead. 'Things were so chaotic downstairs I wondered if it would ever reach us.'

The top buttons of his shirt had been left undone, and its pale material threw into sharp contrast the tanned skin it revealed. He brought an aura of cool cleanliness with him that was almost tangible, and totally masculine.

No matter what he was or was not wearing, Paige thought, her throat tightening, there was no denying his sheer physicality. Or his attraction.

She pointed to the trolley. 'What is all this?'

'Siege rations.'

'I was referring,' she said, 'to the champagne and candles.'

'I thought you'd probably be in need of a tonic after the rigours of the past few hours. Champagne's the best reviver I know—at least in liquid form. The candles are for the moment the power goes off.' He slanted a grin at her. 'Or did you think I was planning a romantic candlelit meal? It's still the middle of the day, you know. And I operate better in the evening.'

Speculation had taken her entirely along those lines, she realised with annoyance. Slightly flushed, she hurried into speech again. 'Do you think it will happen?'

'Which? Dinner *à deux* or the electricity?'

Her colour deepened. 'The power failure, naturally.'

Nick shrugged. 'It has been known, and the alternative supply is a temperamental generator, so the hotel makes emergency provision.'

'None of this,' she said, looking apprehensively towards the shutters as the wind threw itself with renewed force against the window, 'sounds very safe.'

'Afraid the hotel will blow away?' he queried lightly. 'Don't be. It's withstood worse than this over the years. That's why so many people tend to use it as a refugee centre.' He smiled again, but more gently. 'You're in no real danger, you know. You're more likely to die of boredom than you are to be whisked away by some whirlwind, I promise you.'

'Yes.' She moved stiff lips in the semblance of a response. 'I'm sure you're right.' She paused. 'Perhaps I will have that shower, after all. While I still can.'

Moving self-consciously, she unzipped her own bag, finding underwear, a pair of white Capri pants and a loose silky overshirt in a rich shade of jade-green. But Nick, as her swift, sideways glance revealed, wasn't taking a blind bit of notice. He'd stretched out on the bed and appeared to be deep in some paperback book.

'Please make yourself at home,' Paige commented icily as she stalked past him to the bathroom.

'Thanks,' he said, without raising his eyes. 'Allow me to extend you the same courtesy.'

A none-too subtle way of reminding her that he was footing the bill and that this was his room, she realised smoulderingly. And his bed.

She was dismayed to discover that the bolt on the bathroom door was not only inadequate in size, but broken too.

He could have mentioned, it, she told herself. But Nick, clearly, did not bother about such niceties. If he'd even noticed.

However, his casual attitude did not alleviate any of her immediate concerns, she thought as she shed her clothes. Nor did his reassurance about her safety. Because she knew that the real danger had nothing at all to do with the weather—but was only a few feet away from her behind a door which she could close, but not lock.

This was the first time they'd been alone in any kind of intimacy since that disaster of a honeymoon, she realised as she stepped under the stream of water. And she'd sworn then that she would never allow it to happen again. That she could not take the risk...

Yet—here she was, through no fault of her own. Although that was proving small consolation.

They said time was a great healer, yet the pain of her memories of that brief time was still there, just below the surface, waiting to strike at her again. To tear her to ribbons.

She felt sudden, unexpected tears prick at her eyes, and lifted her face to the water to wash away the telltale evidence of distress.

Because this was a secret wound, she thought. And one that she had to conceal from Nick at all costs.

Wasn't that why she'd gone out of her way to evade him all these long months?

She switched off the water and pushed open the door of the cubicle. There was a mirror on the tiled wall directly opposite, and for a moment she stood, almost blankly, staring at herself. At her ungiven, unwanted body.

Not just slender, she thought, but *thin*. Hollows at the base of her throat, narrow waist, stomach almost concave, hipbones sharp and without grace.

This—*this* was what Nick had seen—and rejected.

Paige Harrington. Undesirable and undesired.

And, as her throat closed in swift, uncontrollable agony, overhead the lights flickered once and went out, leaving her stranded in pitch darkness.

She'd known it might happen, but she could do nothing to prevent herself crying out in sudden, instinctive alarm. She stood frozen, scared to take even one step. Afraid of tripping on the edge of the cubicle, of slipping on the wet floor beyond and hurting herself. Unable in the impenetrable blackness to see, or hear, or even think clearly. Smothering.

She heard the door open. Nick's voice saying, 'Paige—are you all right?'

'Yes.' Her voice wobbled. 'But I'm stuck here. It's so stupid. I—I dare not move.'

'Wait a moment. I'll light one of the candles...'

'*No.*' It was a wail of distress, involuntary and self-betraying. 'No—you can't.'

There was a pause, then he said, 'Well, I need to get you out of there somehow. Are you still in the shower itself?'

'Yes.' She was gripping the edge of the door so tightly that her fingers hurt.

'Then reach out your hand and I'll come to you.'

No. This time the negation was silent but no less heart-felt.

She swallowed. 'I'd rather wait. Maybe it's just a temporary thing…'

'You mean like our truce?' There was a caustic note in his voice. 'Don't be a fool. You can't stand there shivering.'

She was aware of movement in front of her. She put out her hand and felt the warmth of his skin under the thin shirt. Frighteningly close.

'Good girl.' His own hand came up and captured her fingers before she could withdraw them. Quivering, she felt him touch her arm, then her shoulder. 'Now, I think this is the easiest way—but for God's sake don't wriggle, because you're wet.'

Before she could utter a word of protest his hands had slid down to her waist and he was clasping her firmly, lifting her against him. Holding her there with one arm as he carried her towards what was now the dim oblong of the doorway.

And there wasn't a damned thing she could do about it, she raged inwardly.

The scent of his skin filled her nose and mouth. The heat of his body seemed to penetrate to her bones. Deep within her she felt the onset of that sweet trembling ache that she'd thought she'd managed to erase for ever.

As an ordeal, it only lasted a few seconds, but it seemed like hours before she felt herself being lowered and encountered the chill of the floor under her bare feet.

She drew a shaking breath. She said on the edge of her voice, 'There was—really—no need for that.'

'Well, there we differ. Didn't you tell me once you hated the dark?'

'Yes,' she admitted unwillingly, surprised that he'd remembered. 'But even so...'

'You were beginning to sound hysterical,' he went on. 'So summary action was needed. I'll find your clothes later,' he added, his tone matter of fact. 'In the meantime make do with this.'

She felt the softness of towelling being placed round her shoulders. 'What is that?' Not, she prayed, another miniature bath towel.

'It's a robe,' he said. 'And, before you ask, it's not mine but the hotel's. Just in case you feared further contamination.'

'Thank you.' Paige thrust her arms into the sleeves and fumbled for the tie belt. 'You make me sound ungrateful,' she went on stiffly. 'And I don't intend to be. I—I'm sure you meant well.'

'Perhaps,' he said softly. 'Or maybe I simply wanted to find out if your skin still felt like smooth, cool silk, and just—seized my chance.'

She wasn't cool any more. She was burning all over with shame, indignation and a mixture of other emotions it might be wiser not to analyse.

Her lips parted in outrage to deliver some blistering comment which would blight the rest of his life. But the right words wouldn't come.

At last, all she could manage was a lame, 'You're despicable.'

He laughed. 'No, darling, I'm an opportunist. That's the secret of my success.' He paused. 'And now, ready or not, I'm going to light some of these candles.'

She stayed where she was, her arms folded across her body in classic defensive posture, watching him inimically as each tiny flame caught, then steadied. He used the saucers from the trolley as candleholders, pouring a little melted wax on to their surfaces to provide a firm grip. He put one on each of the night tables flanking the bed, another on the dressing chest, and the fourth on the trolley itself.

'There,' he said softly when he'd finished. 'The perfect setting for a cosy meal and a pleasant domestic chat.'

It would have given her infinite pleasure to tell him she wasn't hungry and what he could do with his food, but it would have been a sour victory because she would simply have ended by watching him eat instead, and she was starving.

Coldly, she took the chair he indicated and accepted the napkin he handed her. Deftly, Nick opened the champagne and poured it into the waiting flutes.

'A toast,' he said, passing her the slender glass, 'to our better understanding.'

Paige sipped reluctantly. 'Is it necessary we have one— for the short time that's left?'

'You speak as if I'm suddenly going to disappear from your life in a puff of smoke.' Nick studied his wine with narrowed eyes. 'Yet, married or divorced, we'll still be involved professionally.'

She shrugged a shoulder. 'Only while you stay at Harringtons, and who can say how long that will be?'

'Planning a palace *coup,* darling?' Nick offered her the sandwiches.

'I simply meant that things are running more smoothly now, and we no longer need your undivided attention,' Paige returned. 'So you'll be able to get back to—whatever you were doing before.'

'Would you like me to tell you what that was?' he asked with faint amusement.

'No.' She finished her sandwich and took another.

'You don't think a wife should take an intelligent interest in her husband's working life?'

'Perhaps,' she said. 'If it's a real marriage. Which doesn't apply in our case.'

'That,' he said softly, 'is true. However, it hasn't stopped me having a look at the way you've been earning a crust over the past year, and I've found it quite fascinating.'

'Thank you,' she said. 'I've had to learn quickly.'

'And you're clearly an apt pupil.'

His mouth seemed to have hardened suddenly, Paige thought. Or was it just the effect of the candlelight?

She hesitated. 'It hasn't always been easy.'

And she could say that again, she thought wryly. Not only had she taken a cut in salary, but there'd been times in the past twelve months when bad publicity had seriously threatened, and she'd felt like the little Dutch boy holding back the floodwaters with his finger in the dam. While Toby seemed to have turned non-communication into an art form, she acknowledged with a touch of grimness.

'Well, we'll have to see what the board can do to lighten your load.'

It should have been a sympathetic response. The words were right, yet it missed by a mile. Or was she imagining the irony she'd picked up in his tone? There seemed to be undercurrents here she did not understand—and there had been since their first confrontation on the beach.

I'm just stressed out, she told herself, and my mind is playing tricks on me.

She drank some more wine, feeling the chill of it caress her throat. She was surely entitled to some nervous reaction, given the current situation. But at the same time it was important to let Nick think she was calm and in control, she reminded herself.

'You're very quiet.' His dark face was quizzical as he studied her.

Paige shrugged. 'I'm not much good with strangers,' she returned with a touch of defiance.

Nick's brows lifted. 'Is that how you see us?'

'Actually,' she said, 'I don't see *us* at all.'

'Nevertheless,' he said, 'I do happen to be part of your life, and will continue to be for the foreseeable future. It occurs to me we'd do well to extend the truce beyond the limits of this room. Look to the future rather than the here and now.'

She said curtly, 'I think the present is as much as I can cope with.'

From somewhere below there was the noise of shouting and the crash of broken glass.

Paige jumped. ''What's happened? Is the storm getting worse?'

Nick shrugged. 'I'd say it's some of the guests, trying to drink themselves into oblivion.' His smile was brief, even wintry. 'You really are better off up here.'

'Naturally you'd think so.' She lifted her chin. 'But I can look after myself.'

He inclined his head courteously. 'Well, let's hope you're never called upon to prove it.' He passed her the plate of flans. 'I suggest you build your strength up—just in case.'

She took one of the savouries, eyeing him mutinously.

They ate and drank in silence for a few moments, then Paige said, 'How long do you think we're going to be—incarcerated like this?'

'Why, darling, has my company begun to pall? I must try to be more entertaining.' He leaned back in his chair. 'Now, what could I suggest, I wonder, to make the next twelve hours pass more quickly?' he mused softly.

He didn't even glance towards the bed. He didn't have to, Paige realised, her heartbeat quickening. The implication was clear in the tone of his voice—the sensuous twist of his mouth.

She had to resist the impulse to draw the lapels of the

robe closer round her throat. She didn't need to betray to this man the sudden havoc he'd created in her senses.

She made herself speak coolly, 'Well, please don't concern yourself on my account.' She paused. 'You don't really think we could be here for another twelve hours—do you?'

'Your guess is as good as mine.' Nick helped himself to the pineapple. 'The original forecast gave us plenty of time to get out of here, but, like most women, Minna is proving unpredictable.'

Her mouth tightened. 'Do we really need the sexist remarks?'

'Probably not,' he said. 'I just enjoy watching you rise to the bait. Surely you won't grudge me that solitary pleasure from our marriage?' he added silkily.

Oh, God, she thought, her throat closing. That was so *unfair*. He was the one who'd drawn back. Who'd established the limits. And she had the scars to prove it. The memory of the deepest humiliation of her life.

And he could *not* have forgotten.

Even so she was not about to remind him.

Restlessly, Paige pushed her chair back and rose.

'Planning a stroll?'

'Only to get my clothes,' she returned shortly.

'Why bother? The robe looks good on you.' His grin mocked the faint colour warming her face.

'I'd prefer to be properly dressed.'

'Feeling vulnerable, darling?' he asked softly. 'Now there's a damaging admission.'

'Nothing of the kind.' Paige kept her voice even. 'But, as you say, it's the middle of the day, and I'm not used to lounging around in a dressing gown at this hour.'

Nick gave her a dry look as he reached for the coffee pot. 'You lounge like a coiled spring,' he said. 'But get dressed by all means, if it makes you feel better.'

'I was not aware,' she said, her voice shaking, 'that I needed your permission.'

'No,' Nick said quietly. 'But my goodwill could be valuable.' He paused. 'Also my forbearance.'

'Is that a threat?' she demanded coldly.

His mouth twisted. 'More a friendly warning, darling. These are unusual circumstances, so don't push me.'

'A situation,' she said, 'of your own contriving.'

'Not guilty, Paige. I don't control the weather.'

'That,' she said, 'can only be an oversight. You seem able to manipulate everything else in the way you want.'

'If that was true,' Nick said slowly, 'I wouldn't have had to wait for Hurricane Minna's intervention in order to be alone with you.'

The words seemed to drop into her consciousness like stones into a pool, the ripples spreading silently and inexorably. Her heart was racing suddenly, and there was a strange quivering in the pit of her stomach as she made herself meet the frank intensity of his gaze. She felt the sudden shocking hardening of her nipples against the soft towelling that covered them.

She said, 'Another excellent reason for me to hate her.'

Then, with an assumption of calm that she was far from feeling, she picked up a candle from the trolley, carried it into the bathroom, and shut the door behind her.

She leaned back against the reassurance of its panels, her breathing shallow and rapid, the knuckles of one hand pressed bruisingly against her mouth as she fought for control.

She was shaking so much that she realised she was in danger of dropping the candle, or at least spilling hot wax down herself. Moving slowly and carefully, she placed the saucer on the shelf above the basin.

She retrieved her clothes from the towel rail and huddled

them on almost frantically. But they were a fragile defence at best, and she knew it.

She was horrified at her own reaction. At her own stupidity. Had she learned nothing from the past? Nothing at all?

Nick did not want her. That was the simple truth—the certainty she needed to hang on to. For reasons she couldn't even begin to fathom he was playing games with her head. But she couldn't afford to let that go on. She would have to put a stop to it somehow, or she might be faced with another moment of agonising self-betrayal.

There was probably, Paige told herself almost detachedly, a measure of sexual pique in his behaviour. It must gall him to find himself married to one of the few women in the world who seemed to find him totally resistible.

That was what had led to the fiasco of their honeymoon, she thought painfully as she brushed her tangled hair back into submission. His arrogant need to prove to himself that she was his for the taking.

Only in the end he hadn't been sufficiently interested to—take.

Leaving her shocked and damaged in the rags of her self-esteem.

'He will never,' she whispered to herself, 'do that to me again.'

On the other hand it was foolish, and could be dangerous, to persist in needling him like that. She didn't need to score points. Or to be punished for doing so, she thought, swallowing.

Her primary aim had to be to get back to England, and normality, relatively unscathed.

Once on her own ground she could deal with Nick Destry, just as she'd done in the past. And once the divorce was safely through she could put him out of her mind for ever and start rebuilding her life.

She stared at herself in the mirror for a moment. In the flicker of the candle flame her face was all hollows and shadows. She looked like her own ghost.

The last thing in the world she wanted was to be alone with Nick again, but this was the hand Fate had dealt her and she'd have to play it to her own best advantage. Neutralise, somehow, this enforced intimacy, and play down the antagonism between them. Pretend, even, that they were on the same side.

She drew a deep, unsteady breath, then reluctantly went back into the bedroom.

Nick was still sprawled in his chair, an untouched coffee cup beside him, his frowning gaze apparently fixed on some distant and disagreeable horizon.

Paige swallowed. 'Nick,' she said. 'Nick—I'm sorry for what I said. It was—unnecessary—and unkind.'

He turned his head slowly and looked at her. 'My God,' he said with a touch of derision. 'What's brought about this change of heart?'

She tried to smile. 'The truth is this storm is scaring me witless. I'm not thinking straight. It was—very considerate of you to arrange this room, and I haven't even thanked you for it.'

'Don't worry about it.' His voice was expressionless. 'We both have things to regret, but fortunately not for much longer.'

'Yes,' she said quickly. 'Yes—that's the only sensible way to look at it.'

'I don't think,' he said, 'that sense has played much part in our dealings with each other so far.' He looked her over measuringly, his eyes lingering on the cropped trousers which emphasised her slender legs, the vivid colour of the shirt, then smiled swiftly and with charm. 'Some security blanket.'

'Oh.' Paige shook her head, fiddling self-consciously

with the jade silk collar. 'I shall only feel really secure when I leave the plane at Heathrow.'

'Of course,' he said, with faint mockery. 'Back to the sanctuary of the family citadel. How the Harringtons do stick together.'

'There's nothing wrong with family loyalty,' Paige said defensively.

Nick shrugged. 'That might depend on how far the bonds are stretched.' He got to his feet. 'I hate to jeopardise this new-found accord, but I think maybe we should conserve the candles. We don't know how much longer we might need them.' He looked at her gravely. 'Can you bear to be in the dark again? It won't cause you any problems?'

She forced a laugh. 'Heavens, no. Anyway, it's such a stupid, childish thing,' she added lightly. 'I should have grown out of it by now.'

'How did it begin?' he asked.

Paige shrugged, to disguise her momentary hesitation. 'I really can't remember,' she lied.

'And you've never seen anyone about it—been offered treatment?'

'No—and anyway it doesn't happen very often these days. It's usually when I find myself in strange surroundings.' She smiled brightly. 'While I stick to the familiar, I'm fine.'

'And when you're not alone.' It was a statement rather than a question, and this time her hesitation was obvious.

'Well, yes—I suppose...'

'Then there's nothing to worry about,' he said. 'Because I'm here, and we'll stick it out together while Minna does her worst.' He paused. 'I suggest you take the bed,' he went on briskly. 'It's more comfortable than these damned chairs, and you might even get some more sleep. Pass the time that way.'

'But what about you?' She tried to sound equally matter of fact, even though alarm bells were ringing.

'I'll be chivalrous,' he returned. 'And risk dislocation of the spine.'

'But you won't even be able to read.'

'It doesn't matter. As it happens, I have some serious thinking to do. A major new investment that I have to consider before I get back. Don't worry—I won't get bored and stray,' he added with a touch of mockery.

'I wasn't…'

'And don't fib,' he went on. 'Because you're lousy at it.'

Yes, she thought. And always had been.

She lay down on top of the covers, watching as he extinguished each tiny flame in turn. When he'd finished she turned on to her side, closing her eyes as he made his way quietly back to his chair.

The roar of the wind showed no sign of lessening. In fact it seemed louder than ever, she thought with an inward sigh. Would they ever get out of here?

She wouldn't sleep, of course. That would be silly. Because she might wake and find herself in unfamiliar darkness. And if she cried out Nick would come to her, as he'd done last time. And the time before that… The time she didn't allow herself to think about.

And that would be fatal.

CHAPTER SEVEN

OUTSIDE, all hell might have broken loose, but inside the room, Paige was aware of a curious stillness, totally divorced from the elements but equally disturbing.

She might almost have been alone, she thought. She couldn't see Nick, or discern any kind of movement, but she knew he was there, only a few feet away, because every sense—every tingling nerve-ending in her body—was telling her so.

She moved slightly, quietly, unwilling to draw attention to herself, burrowing deeper into the mattress as if she was trying to make herself invisible. Or at any rate to hide. To render herself equally unobtrusive.

The room, at least, no longer seemed an alien environment to her. She could, if pushed, describe every tile on the floor, the colours in the fabrics and each stick of furniture, she thought wryly. A few more hours there and she'd probably be carving her name on the walls. And climbing them, too.

She should try to relax, she knew. Even sleep. It was the only way to endure the hours of waiting for the hurricane to pass. But she was just too aware of Nick's proximity.

A silent presence, icily concentrated, as he planned the next big deal, she told herself. And when it was done other lives would probably change for ever, just as hers had done.

She should, of course, have refused to accompany Nick to Normandy. Made it crystal-clear that any form of honeymoon was preposterous—unthinkable. Even at the airport it would not have been too late. She could simply have walked away and booked a cab back to London.

So why didn't I? she thought, biting her lip. Fear of the inevitable scene—the possible repercussions? Well, maybe, but if she was honest there had been another factor in the equation by then, sparked off by the memory of that astonishing kiss. And the fact that he'd not attempted even the most casual of follow-ups.

Curiosity, she told herself wryly, with hindsight. That was what it had been. And a certain amount of pique— both totally female and highly dangerous.

Although at the time she'd pretended to herself that it was Normandy itself, which she'd never visited before, that intrigued her—and Madame de Charrier's family home. And that, of course, had been the first major surprise.

When Nick had said his grandmother had returned to her former village Paige had visualised a tall, narrow house in some quiet street behind the church, within easy reach of the *boulangerie*.

She had not been prepared for the gracious grey-stoned mansion standing proudly at the end of its own avenue of trees.

'It's very quiet here,' Nick said almost curtly as Antoine, the elderly man who'd met them at the airport, brought the car to a halt in front of the heavily timbered front door. 'I thought we could both do with some peace—and some space. But if you really hate it we can always go on to Paris.'

She said, 'It's beautiful,' and meant it. 'And incredibly big.'

'Yes,' he agreed cordially. 'With any luck we can spend the entire week without setting eyes on each other once.'

She said, 'Yes,' in a subdued voice. She had wanted but not dared to ask about the sleeping arrangements, but Nick's comment gave her a vague reassurance.

As she got out of the car a plump woman erupted from the house, wreathed in smiles.

'Hortense, my grandmother's housekeeper,' Nick said in an undertone, before he was overwhelmed in a voluble, clucking embrace to which he laughingly submitted.

When it was her turn Paige found herself being swiftly assessed by dark twinkling eyes.

'Too thin,' was the brisk verdict from Madame Marquay. She nodded emphatically. 'We must feed her well, so that she will have strong babies.'

Paige, crimson, marched into the house, avoiding Nick's sardonic glance. That, she thought, smouldering, was the trouble with faithful family retainers. They tended to be outspoken.

She soon discovered that Hortense was indeed the lynch-pin of the establishment. With the help of local women, whom she chivvied unmercifully, she kept the house in pristine condition and produced long and delicious meals, while Antoine, her long-suffering husband, worked the same miracle in the grounds with his own band of helpers. In his spare time, Hortense said proudly, he made the best calvados in the region.

To Paige's relief, the housekeeper made no overtly dis-approving comment when she showed her to the grand first-floor bedroom, with its huge *lit matrimoniale* enticingly made up with crisp, snowy bedlinen redolent of lavender, which she was to occupy in solitary splendour, and then indicated the adjoining room which had been prepared for Nick. But her silence spoke volumes. Clearly in *madame's* view newly married couples slept in each others' arms, not separate rooms.

As far as Paige was concerned Nick's presence on the other side of a substantial wall was still far too near, but that was not something she could tell his devoted Hortense.

The few clothes she'd brought with her looked lost in the cavernous *armoire*, but she was glad she'd included a swimsuit when Nick showed her the luxurious pool, complete with fountain, which had been built at the rear of the house.

'Your grandmother had this done?' she asked, surprised.

Nick shook his head. 'Before she moved back here she had some wealthy Americans as longstanding tenants. All Grandmère did was give her permission, *et voilà*.'

Voilà indeed, Paige thought, assimilating with wonder the expensively tiled surround and the circular changing pavilion constructed from the same stone as the house itself. Thank God Denise can't see this, or the diggers would be at the Hall tomorrow.

'Dinner will be at eight,' he went on. 'And I shall expect you to join me for it.'

'Is that really necessary? I—I'm not very hungry.'

His glance measured her coldly. 'And you also have a headache, plus terminal fatigue from the journey, right?' He shook his head. 'Forget it, Paige. This happens to be our wedding night, and Hortense will have gone to a lot of trouble to cook us a special dinner to celebrate. You won't be asked to comply with any of the other wifely obligations due to the occasion,' he added bitingly, 'but you'll damned well turn up for meals and be civil.' He paused. 'Do I make myself clear?'

Their eyes met—clashed. But Paige was the first to look away, her throat muscles tightening nervously.

She said huskily, 'As crystal.' Then turned and marched away from him, aware that her heart was beating rapidly and that there were tears pricking at her eyelids. Tears of anger, she told herself defiantly. But certainly not disappointment. Never—ever—that…

After that she expected the honeymoon to be an ongoing nightmare of awkwardness and embarrassment, yet, strangely, it was not—even though that first meal together was, inevitably, a strained and difficult occasion. The panelled formality of the dining room felt slightly oppressive too.

But, in spite of her professed loss of appetite, Paige found it impossible to resist Hortense's exquisite casserole of chicken, simmered with apples and calvados, or the tiny raspberry soufflés which followed it. And perhaps Nick's excellent choice of wines helped too.

Over the meal he talked casually and pleasantly on general topics, seemingly unfazed by her monosyllabic replies.

And he made no effort to detain her when she finished her coffee and rose, mumbling something incoherent about an early night.

'Goodnight, Paige.' His smile was coolly polite. 'Sleep well.'

'Thank you,' she managed, and escaped.

The communicating door between their rooms was now locked, she discovered when she tentatively tried it. But it was less reassuring to find that the key was not on her side.

She was genuinely tired, but she lay wide awake and tense, waiting for the telltale glimmer of light to appear at the foot of the door, signalling that Nick too had retired for the night.

And even when it disappeared, and there was only the moonlight spilling through the slats in the tall shuttered windows across the wooden floor, it was nearly an hour before Paige felt secure enough to close her eyes and compose herself for sleep.

She awoke to brilliant sunshine, and croissants with rich cherry jam and a bowl of *café au lait* served to her on the terrace.

Monsieur, Hortense told her, lips slightly pursed, had breakfasted earlier and taken the car to Caen. He would return in time for lunch.

So she was left to her own devices, Paige realised a trifle blankly. Nick must have meant what he'd said about them keeping their distance from each other. Which, of course, was exactly what she wanted.

Nevertheless, she felt slightly at a loss as she wandered round, trying to familiarise herself a little with the house. The dining room might have been rather too forbidding for her taste, but she loved the big, airy *salon,* with its enormous fireplace. This was empty now, of course, but she could imagine it ablaze with logs when the winter mists and rain closed in, as Nick had told her they could.

The sofas and chairs had been chosen with an eye to comfort rather than grandeur, so, in spite of its size, there was an essential homeyness about the room which appealed to Paige.

She guessed that one imposing high-backed *fauteuil,* placed near the fire, belonged to Madame de Charrier when she was in residence. There was a small round table beside it, with a hinged top, and when Paige raised the lid she realised it was a sewing table. There was a piece of half-finished embroidery inside, with fabulously overblown roses on a background of cream linen. It was exquisite, Paige thought, gently touching the delicate stitches.

She heard a faint sound, and turned to find Nick standing in the doorway, watching her. His brows were slightly raised and he was smiling.

'Oh.' Paige swallowed, hastily replacing the embroidery and closing the lid. 'I—I didn't realise you were back.'

'Caen was hot and crowded. I decided to come back early and get in a swim before lunch.' He paused. 'Would you like to join me?'

It was on the tip of her tongue to refuse. To reinforce the policy of avoidance that he'd established.

Instead, incredibly, she heard herself say, 'That would be—nice.'

'Good.' His tone was casual. 'Then I'll see you down at the pool.' He threw her a swift smile and disappeared.

Paige stood very still, aware that her breathing had quickened.

Not, she thought, the wisest decision she'd ever made. But she could always remain where she was—tell him that she'd changed her mind. Only she didn't want to give him the impression that she found his company disturbing—did she? Or that she was scared to join him?

She needed to copy his own laid-back attitude, she decided. Indicate her own indifference to his presence.

After all, she told herself with an inward shrug, it *was* only a swim. And went upstairs to change.

Nick was already in the pool when she arrived, and she felt self-conscious as she slipped off her wrap, aware that her plain black one-piece, cut high on the leg and square across her breasts, was the least she'd ever worn in front of him.

But once she was in the water too, her strong graceful sidestroke carrying her swiftly from one end of the pool to the other and back, she forgot everything but the sheer enjoyment of the moment. Nick came to swim beside her, not competing, but slowing his own powerful pace to match hers. And somehow that was all right too.

At last she clung, laughing and breathless, to the side of the pool. 'That was terrific.'

He grinned, pushing his wet hair back from his forehead. 'This is where I thought I'd find you when I came back. How did you manage to resist for so long?'

'I enjoyed looking round the house,' Paige countered. 'It's an amazing place. Is it very old?'

'Parts of it. It was certainly here when Henry the Fifth paid his memorable visit. But it survived that, and the Revolution later. And somehow it came through the last war, although it was occupied by the Germans, and afterwards the British and Americans.' He paused. 'You should ask Grandmère to tell you about it some time. She was a young girl then, but she was mixed up with the local Résistance and she's got some incredible stories from that time.'

'Yes.' Paige remembered the ramrod back and gimlet gaze. 'I'm sure she has.' She shook her head. 'I don't think I'd have been very brave.'

'Yet you've just married a complete stranger,' Nick said softly. 'A lot of people would think that's insanely courageous.'

She hunched a defensive shoulder. 'Or just insane. And, after all, it isn't a real marriage,' she added hastily.

'Thank you for reminding me,' he said courteously. 'But it wasn't necessary. I'm not likely to forget.'

There was a silence, tense and tingling, as if an electric current had passed through the water between them, then Nick pulled himself out of the pool in one swift, lithe movement and reached for his towel. 'It's nearly time for lunch,' he tossed casually over his shoulder. 'We'd better not keep Hortense waiting.'

Paige had one mesmerising, mouth-drying glimpse of the lean muscularity of his body, barely concealed by the brief trunks he was wearing, then turned and began to swim slowly back to the other end, where she'd left her own things.

From now on, she thought, it might be safer to take her own swim when Nick was out of the way.

But as the hours began to measure themselves slowly in days Paige found she was becoming more relaxed. Even, if it were possible, beginning to enjoy herself.

True, Nick was away from the house for most of every day, but it wasn't long before she found herself beginning to time his return, listening for his voice in the hall, the sound of his step on the flagged floors. She took care never to ask where he'd been, or comment if he was delayed, and he never offered an explanation for his absences.

And, instead of being something to avoid, the pre-lunch swim became part of the fabric of her existence—something to be anticipated, even relished.

So when, on the fifth day, Nick said he had business at the bank in the nearby town, and asked if she'd like to go with him to look round the market, she heard herself accept equally casually.

Nick parked on some waste ground near the church, and walked with her through a maze of narrow streets to the centre of the town.

The market square was crowded, with local people mingling with tourists as they clustered round the stalls.

'The bank's over there.' Nick pointed. 'I won't be long.'

'Where shall I meet you?'

'Don't worry about it.' His tone was laconic. 'I'll find you.'

'In this mass of people?'

His mouth twisted. He said softly, 'Anywhere.' His fingers brushed her cheek lightly, but she felt his touch shiver in her blood, and knew that what he said was true.

She watched him go, shouldering his way through the crowd. Waited until he was out of sight before she moved, plunging blindly into the horde of people, with no idea where she was heading.

I wish he hadn't said that, she whispered silently, wrapping her arms across her body. Or done that.

The market seemed to sell everything from pots and pans to handmade jewellery, from brushes and shovels to curtains.

You could probably set up home in an hour, Paige thought as she wandered about aimlessly. She could feel the blaze of the sun on her head, and paused to buy herself a hat, broad-brimmed and floppy in unbleached linen.

But the main speciality was, naturally, food, and she guessed that all the holidaymakers staying in the vicinity had converged on the market to buy fresh meat and vegetables to take back to their *gîtes*.

That would be fun, she thought, pausing to stare at piles of gleaming tomatoes and bunches of tiny radishes, and noticing, with a sudden odd wistfulness, a young couple, hand in hand and smiling into each other's eyes as they made their choice.

Fun to plan a meal and saunter round in the sunlight collecting the ingredients for it in leisurely contentment. To prepare it together, then share it with a bottle of wine as the moon rose. And, afterwards, make love…

She swallowed nervously and turned away. But the nagging thought persisted that if she and Nick had met on different terms—enjoyed a normal relationship—then she would undoubtedly have cooked him a meal or several by now. And drunk with him to their future.

And slept with him too…

She found her fingers straying to the cheek he had touched, and stopped with a stifled gasp, firmly burying her hands in the pockets of her sleeveless blue dress.

I must learn, she told herself grimly, not to let my imagination run away with me.

Her attention not entirely focused on where she was going, she suddenly cannoned into someone. Firm hands gripped her arms, steadying her as she instinctively recoiled.

She looked up and met Nick's amused gaze. 'I told you I'd find you,' he said.

'Oh.' She freed herself swiftly, struggling for composure. 'I—I didn't see you.'

'Or hear me either,' he said drily. 'I called to you twice.'

'I—I was miles away. Daydreaming.'

'So I gathered.' He paused, his eyes dwelling thoughtfully on her flushed face. 'I hope it was a nice dream.'

No, she thought. Not nice at all. *Dangerous*.

She forced a smile. 'Rather culinary and domestic, actually.'

His brows lifted. 'That's the right kind of dream for a Frenchman's wife to have.'

'You're hardly French.'

'You don't think so?' His swift shrug was totally Gallic. 'Well, never say that to Grandmère. She wouldn't agree.' He paused. 'I like the hat. But I hope it's waterproof because there's rain on the way.'

Paige looked up at the cloudless sky, relieved at the change to an impersonal topic. 'Surely not.'

'Alas, yes. This is Normandy, remember, not the Riviera.' He gave her a considering look. 'Why don't we have some lunch, and go to the coast before the weather breaks? After all, you haven't seen any of the countryside yet.' He paused. 'Or would you rather go back to the house?'

'No.' Paige met his gaze steadily. 'I'd like to see the coast. But, instead of going to a restaurant, why don't we *buy* our lunch and take it with us?'

'Thrifty too,' Nick murmured, his eyes glinting wickedly. 'Take care, Mrs Destry, or you could turn into the perfect wife.'

She flushed and turned away.

They bought baguettes and sliced ham, smoked sausage, some mild yellow cheese, and a bag of the tomatoes she'd admired earlier, adding two large bottles of mineral water to their haul.

'Are we going to one of the famous beaches from the D-Day landings?' Paige asked as she sat beside him in the car.

'Not this time.' He shot her a swift glance. 'They're incredible, but they can be overwhelming too. And tragic. So I thought today we'd simply relax and enjoy ourselves instead, and save the sightseeing for another time.'

'Fine,' she assented quietly. *So, there was going to be another time. And should she be pleased—or wary?*

She was still pondering this dilemma when Nick brought the car to a halt under the shade of a tree.

'From here we walk,' he said.

The grass was short and crisp under their feet, and ahead of them was the Channel, blue and serene today.

'The path's over here,' Nick directed. 'It's a bit steep in places, so I'll go first.'

He wasn't joking, Paige realised breathlessly as she picked her way gingerly down the rocky slope. She slid the last couple of feet, landing in soft sand, laughing with delight as she dusted herself down.

It was only a small cove, guarded on each side by high rocks, but it breathed tranquillity. They didn't have it to themselves either. Several windbreaks had been set up along the beach, and there were small children playing at the water's edge.

Nick had brought a rug from the car, and spread it in the shelter of a large boulder.

Paige sat down, looking enviously at the gentle ripple of the water. 'I wish I'd brought my swimsuit.'

'You're better off sticking to the pool.' Nick was unpacking the food. 'The sea never gets that warm here, and there are quite nasty currents further out.'

'You clearly know it well.'

'I spent most of my holidays in Normandy when I was a child. I used to come here with my parents—and Grandmère too. It was our favourite place.'

She felt startled, yet oddly gratified that he'd chosen to bring her to it. She covered her momentary confusion by saying quickly, 'Your grandmother came down that path?'

'She used to come down it in the dark years ago,' he said quietly. 'When boats were being landed here.'

'I suppose so.' Paige hunched a shoulder. 'It's not as peaceful here as I thought,' she added wryly. 'It has its own ghosts.'

Nick grinned and passed her a chunk of bread and some ham. 'You're just hungry.'

He was right, she discovered to her surprise. She was ravenous. And it was a wonderful meal—sticky and messy, with crumbs and sand everywhere. And with Nick, she acknowledged wonderingly, easier company than she'd ever known him.

For the first time she was able to drop her guard. To find again the person she'd ceased to be the evening her father had told her falteringly what was expected of her.

Perhaps, in some strange way, she and Nick might even become friends, she told herself, trying and failing to raise some enthusiasm at the prospect.

When they'd finished their picnic Paige went to rinse her hands in the sea. On her return she found Nick had stripped off his shirt and stretched out on the rug, his eyes closed.

Cautiously she sat down on the opposite side of the rug. She undid the top two buttons on her dress and slid down the straps, baring her shoulders, then folded back her skirt to a decorous mid-thigh level.

Of course she wouldn't go to sleep, she told herself as she lay down. There were too many thoughts chasing themselves round in her head for that. Too many unlooked for emotions seething inside her.

She was bewildered at her own frank enjoyment of the day's simple pleasures. And concerned at how dangerously easy it had been to respond to Nick's companionship. They'd talked like ordinary people, and laughed too. He'd teased her, and she'd tossed a retort back at him.

She turned her head warily, and looked at him from under her lashes. There was no questioning the force of his attraction. Every pulse, every nerve-ending was registering it with pathetic eagerness.

She felt as if, quite unaware, she'd taken a step into the unknown—and there was no turning back.

And it occurred to her, too, that even if Nick were to offer friendship that would no longer be enough.

She knew that was absurd, as well as seriously perilous, and that she should be fighting it with all the intellectual weapons at her disposal, but the sun was so warm on her skin, and the lap of the waves on the shore so soothing. She could hear, in some far distance, the cry of gulls and the laughter of the children. And then that also faded.

She was eventually awoken by something thudding against her ankle. She sat up groggily and stared around her. Her assailant, she saw at once, was a large coloured ball, and tottering to retrieve it was a very small girl in a sunbonnet and frilled knickers. The mite paused at a safe distance and offered an ingratiating smile.

'*Tu veux, petite?*' Gently, Paige rolled it back to her.

The smile widened, revealing an array of small pearly teeth. Then the ball was kicked towards her again with real vigour.

'Hey.' Laughing, Paige stopped it from crashing into the remains of the picnic. 'Pick on someone your own size.'

She batted it back and the baby caught it, clumsily but gleefully trapping it against her rounded tummy.

'Oh, well done.' Paige clapped the feat. 'Bravo.'

'Simone.' It was Maman, coming in search of her errant offspring. '*Qu'est ce que tu fais ici, mignonne? Mille pardons M'sieu—'dame.*'

Paige looked round quickly and saw that Nick was propped up on one elbow, staring at her. There was an odd, almost frozen expression on his face, and his mouth had thinned to a hard line.

He looked, she thought, almost angry. But why?

'Oh, did we wake you? I'm sorry.' She smiled at him eagerly, placatingly. 'But she was so adorable.'

'I was awake already.' He didn't return her smile, but sat up, reaching for his shirt. 'I think we should be going. That change in the weather is on its way.'

Looking where he indicated, Paige saw a bank of dark cloud building ominously.

'Oh.' She felt ludicrously disappointed at the curtailment of her day. 'What a shame.'

'Why, Paige,' he said mockingly, 'aren't you desperate to get back to sanctuary?'

The camaraderie of the past hours might never have existed, she realised with a pang.

She lifted her chin. 'On the contrary, I feel as if my "Get out of Jail" card has just expired.' And saw his eyes flash angrily as he turned away.

They packed up the debris of the meal they'd shared so light-heartedly, and walked up the beach. Paige scrambled barefoot up the path, ignoring Nick's extended hand.

They didn't exchange a word on the drive back. When they reached the house Paige went straight up to her room. She found Hortense in the passage, with armfuls of clean bedding for the linen room.

'I shan't want any dinner tonight, Hortense.' She bit her lip. 'I—I've got a headache. I think there must be a storm coming.'

'*Mais oui, madame.* I feel it too.' Hortense gave her a compassionate look. 'May I bring you one of my special *tisanes*, perhaps?'

'Thanks, but I don't need a thing.' As she closed her bedroom door behind her Paige was aware that her headache wasn't complete fiction. But not brought on by the weather, she thought furiously. Oh, no. The real cause was the sheer stress of refraining from slapping Nick hard, and bursting into tears for an encore.

The air in the room felt chill suddenly. She closed her window and fastened the shutter, noting, with a grimace, that the sky looked like ink.

She looked in her bag and found the little foil sheet of painkillers, taking two of them. If nothing else, they should knock her out for the duration.

She had a cool bath, then slipped on a fresh nightgown and got into bed.

She'd half expected Nick to come hammering on the door, demanding that she present herself at the dinner table, but there was no sign of him.

Presumably a few hours of her undiluted company was as much as he could take, she thought, feeling the threatened tears pricking absurdly at her eyelids.

Well, that suited her just fine. And maybe she could arrange with Hortense to have all her meals in her room while she remained in this benighted place.

She closed her eyes with determination, but it was some time before the painkillers worked their usual magic and she drifted restlessly into sleep.

It was a strange sleep, too, where she dreamed she was running through the house, going down unrecognisable passages and discovering rooms she had never seen before. And all of them empty. Empty…

She sat up with a sudden start. In the distance there was the sour grumble of thunder, but she was looking into darkness, pitch-black and stifling. For a moment the dream still possessed her, with its labyrinth of emptiness, leaving her shaking—totally disorientated. Her hand reached out, groping for the switch on the bedside lamp in her own room back home and finding—nothing.

Where am I? she thought wildly. What's happening to me?

The darkness pressed on her, filling her mouth, squeezing down into her lungs so she could scarcely breathe.

It was the worst nightmare—a kind of death—and she screamed out loud in panic and protest, her voice high and terrified.

The thunder growled again, and this time there was another noise accompanying it, but closer at hand. The sound of a door opening. And then there was light splintering the darkness, putting it to flight, making her sob in sheer relief.

'Paige?' Nick's voice was sharp with concern. 'In God's name, what is it?'

He switched on the elusive bedside light and sat down beside her, drawing her trembling body into his arms.

'It was dark,' she managed at last, through chattering teeth. 'So dark, and I couldn't find the lamp. And I hate it. I hate finding myself in darkness—not knowing where I am. I—I always have.'

'Well, there's light now,' he said. 'And you're safe.'

Her head was resting against his shoulder and he was stroking her hair with a gentle hand. His skin was cool through the silk of his robe, and fragrant with the fresh, clean scent of soap. There was no darkness where he was, or suffocation, she thought. She could have breathed him for ever.

'Though I can't do much about the storm,' he went on. 'But we've had the worst of it, I think.' He poured her some mineral water from the carafe beside the bed. 'Here, drink this.' He paused while she complied, her dry throat grateful for the coolness. 'Can I get you anything else? A cup of tea, maybe?'

'No.' Her hand clutched his sleeve. 'Don't leave me—please.'

Their eyes met—held. There was a silence, then he said quietly, 'Paige, you know that I must. I can't stay here.'

'But I don't want to be alone. I had this awful dream—all these empty rooms—and then the darkness.'

'The rooms aren't empty,' he said. 'Because I'm in the one next to you, and if the darkness comes back all you have to do is call me. Now try to rest.'

She shook her head. 'I can't.' She took his hand and carried it to her breast. Held it there. 'My heart's still racing.'

'I feel it.' In the lamplight his face was taut, all planes and angles.

'Then how can you leave me?'

'Because,' he said, 'of a promise I made.'

She was suddenly trembling, but not with fear. That had been replaced by an excitement bordering on exultation.

She put up a hand and touched his face, her fingers shy as they lingered on his skin. She whispered, 'I absolve you…'

'Paige.' The name seemed wrung out of him. 'Ah, dear God.'

She lay back against the pillows and he followed her down, his thumb gently tracing the outline of her parted lips.

He said softly, 'I was watching you on the beach this afternoon while you slept. Wondering what it would be like to do this…' He slipped down the lacy straps of her nightgown. 'And this…' He slid the silken bodice away from her breasts, baring them to the hunger of his eyes—and, she discovered, gasping, his mouth.

His lips caressed and adored each delicate scented mound in turn, coaxing the rosy nipples to pucker and harden as his tongue circled them in languid sensuality.

Paige heard herself moan under the force of a pleasure so intense it was almost pain. Her head fell back and her whole body arched in a longing she had never known before. That she had never believed could exist.

And when his lips returned to hers, kissing her deeply, sensuously, his fingers continued the delicious torment of her breasts, stroking and fondling the aroused peaks.

The storm hadn't passed, she thought dazedly. It was here in this room, in this bed, raging in her blood, her pulses echoing the tumult of the thunder.

From the moment of that first kiss her body had been longing for this, her senses on fire. She could deny it no longer.

Her hands parted his robe, pushing it from his shoulders. He was naked beneath it, as she'd always known he would be, and her hands moved on him feverishly, learning the strength of bone and the play of muscle as their mouths teased and sucked and tore.

Nick's breathing was harsh and ragged as his hands explored her in turn, brushing aside her nightgown as if it was a cobweb.

His fingers cupped the curve of her hip, then slid down to part her pliant thighs and master the secret, scalding heat of her.

Her whole body shuddered with pleasure at his touch. She heard her voice, small, driven, say, 'Yes—oh, yes...'

And knew at that moment that everything had suddenly, shockingly, changed. Felt him rear back from her almost violently. Distance himself.

Paige's eyes flew open. His back was turned to her, slicked with sweat. He was reaching for his robe and dragging it on, tightening the belt round his waist with swift, angry emphasis.

'Nick? What is it?' Her whisper cracked in the middle. 'Is something wrong?'

'Just about everything, I'd say. Wouldn't you?' The face he turned to her was a mask, cold and remote.

'I don't understand...'

'It's quite simple.' He sounded like a polite stranger. He

shrugged. 'I thought I could do this—but I can't.' He took the rumpled sheet and drew it across her body. Covering her. Making his rejection of her complete. And frighteningly final. 'I'm sorry.'

'*Sorry?*' She hadn't realised it was possible to feel such pain—such shame. It was a knife being twisted inside her—by the hand of an expert.

And she had invited this. Had brought it upon herself. Something she would never be able to forget. Or forgive.

She thought, I want to die...

She huddled further into the mattress, wishing she could escape, or at least make herself invisible.

She hardly recognised her own voice. 'I—think you'd better go.'

'Yes,' Nick said quietly. 'I think so too.'

She closed her eyes again. She could not bear to watch him walk away. To have her humiliation redefined like that.

When she heard the door close quietly she released her indrawn breath with a little sob, stifled against her clenched fist.

He was wrong about her dream, she thought, as the first tears began to burn in her eyes. All the rooms were empty. And her heart was the emptiest of all.

CHAPTER EIGHT

EVEN after all these months the memory still had the power to sear her to the bone. She had carried it with her like a wound that refused to heal. A potent, burning reminder of her own stupidity.

And of a mistake she had sworn she would never make again.

Yet here she was once more, alone with Nick in the darkness while another storm raged outside. Only the location had changed. And he wasn't on the other side of a closed door this time either.

In spite of her high resolve to shun him, a crazy mischance had condemned her to his company. All she'd managed, she thought bitterly, was to come full circle. It was almost funny, so why wasn't she laughing?

Yet it could have been avoided. She could have taken the job Brad offered, made it clear that theirs would only be a business relationship, and waited out the months for her divorce on St Antoine in comparative peace.

That was, of course, if Nick would have allowed such a thing.

'I haven't finished with you.' That was what he'd said on the beach—was it only last night? Already it seemed like several lifetimes ago. He'd promised to play no more games, but those words still haunted her.

Had he been speaking personally or professionally? she wondered restively.

Whatever, she should have faced up to him—made him explain himself. Because if she was going home to more trouble, as seemed only too likely, then she needed to know about it. Forewarned, after all, was forearmed.

But a serious talk with Toby seemed inevitable. For one thing she needed to tell him that her job with Harringtons just wasn't working out, and that she'd be looking for alternative employment almost at once.

She needed to change her life. To slough off the past year and begin again. She might even go abroad, she thought, but not back here to the Caribbean. In her heart she knew that would not be a sensible move—and not fair on Brad, either, who would always hope for more than she could ever give him.

A friend of hers had spent a year in Australia on an exchange with a journalist working on a Sydney-based magazine. Maybe she could arrange something like that.

But it was hard to be positive when you felt sick and numb. When all you could really think about was the man, silent in the darkness, only a few feet away.

The non-husband who had somehow forced his way back into her consciousness and her life.

She moved restlessly, seeking a cool place on the pillow.

'Are you all right?' He spoke quietly and Paige froze, then invented a sleepy murmur. He'd heard her, even above the noise of the storm.

It was disturbing to think that Nick might be as aware of her as she was of him. And she didn't need his concern—his compassion—now, any more than she'd done a year ago.

She hadn't slept at all for the rest of the night, she recalled. She'd found her nightgown and dragged it on, and lain under the covers, her arms wrapped round her shivering body.

Suddenly the darkness she hated had seemed almost friendly. Because what was she going to do when she had to face Nick in daylight? When they would both have to remember how she'd offered herself to him, naked and willing, only to be rejected?

She had crammed the corner of the sheet into her mouth to stifle the racking sobs threatening to overwhelm her.

Exhausted, she'd finally fallen into an uneasy doze around dawn.

And when she'd awoken, it had been to find Nick standing beside her bed with a tray. As their eyes had met Paige had had to quell an impulse to shrink back under the covers.

No, she thought. I can't let him see that it matters so much.

He said, 'I told Hortense the storm had disturbed you and she was to let you sleep, but it's getting quite late, so I've brought you coffee and rolls.'

'Thank you.' Paige rallied her defences. Kept her tone crisp. 'Please leave the tray somewhere.'

'And get out?' Nick supplied wryly. He shook his head. 'It's not that simple. And the food was just an excuse, anyway.' His mouth tightened. 'We need to talk.'

The breath caught in her throat. 'We've already said everything we need to say. Now I just want to end this farce and go home.'

He was frowning. 'You're leaving?'

'Yes,' she said. 'And today, for preference, if you can arrange a flight or a ferry for me.' She paused. 'Feel free to make up some story to pacify Hortense—and your grandmother. A family illness, perhaps.'

'I'll take you...'

'No.' The word almost exploded out of her. She saw the shock in his face and made herself speak more calmly. 'I'd be grateful if you'd just do as I ask. In fact, I insist.'

There was a long silence, then Nick said quietly, 'Very well.' And went.

And he did everything she asked. He found her a seat on a plane and instructed Antoine to drive her to the airport.

In spite of this, their leavetaking had an inevitable awkwardness. Under Hortense's gimlet gaze, Nick brushed Paige's cheek with his lips in a brief, formal gesture.

His smile didn't reach his eyes. *'Au revoir.'* He paused. 'I'll see you soon.'

'No,' Paige whispered under her breath as she went out to the car. 'No, you won't.'

It had been a resolve born out of desperate necessity and forged in steel. And she'd kept to it throughout the weeks and months which followed. Using it to grind the memory of Nick out of her heart and mind. To erase, she'd hoped for ever, the pained remembrance of her body's half-crazed response to the touch of his hands and mouth. The way she woke, aching for him, in the night. The image of him, his eyes smiling at her, which came to crucify her days.

So many times she'd thought she saw him—passing on the other side of the street, or across a crowded restaurant. And she had come to a halt, her heart juddering, her hands clammy with sudden panic, telling herself that it was nothing but her imagination playing tricks.

Oh, it had been a long, bitter battle, but one she had been beginning to win. Or so she'd thought.

Yet now, thanks to a series of cruel coincidences, she would have to start the whole weary process all over again.

Paige pressed her knuckles against her teeth. She thought, I can't bear it. Oh, dear God, why did this have to happen?

It was madness and she knew it—this fixation with Nick. How could she be so obsessive over someone she'd encountered over the course of only a few weeks? Someone she didn't know in any real sense at all. And who'd made it patently clear he had no interest in her.

Well, she could do it, she told herself, biting her lip until she tasted blood. She could climb the mountain once more. Block from her brain the turn of his head, the tone of his voice, the evocative male scent of him each time they returned to torment her. And they would return, because they always did.

But one day she would be free of them, however long it might take. She had to believe that. Had to. Because anything else really would be madness.

She began to breathe deeply and quietly, practising the relaxation exercises she'd learned, contracting each and every muscle from her toes to the top of her head, then releasing them.

And gradually the images in her head lost their edge and became blurred, until at last they slid away altogether, taking her with them, over the brink into sleep.

When she awoke she was immediately aware of two things. First that the roar of the wind had gone, and it was oddly quiet. Second that there was a weight across her body pinning her to the bed.

For a horrified moment she thought that the hotel might have been structurally damaged, and that part of the ceiling had fallen.

Then she realised, with even more horror, that the weight was warm, and breathing.

Scarcely daring to breathe herself, Paige turned her head slowly and gingerly, only to have her worst fears confirmed.

Nick was lying on the bed behind her, fast asleep, his arm wrapped round her, one leg casually flung across hers, so that she was in virtual imprisonment.

For a moment she was totally still, her body rigid with shock and disbelief. How could this have happened? she wondered wildly. How could he have joined her on the bed like this—and she not know? And when had this—intimate entwining taken place?

The fact that they were both fully dressed seemed little reassurance.

Oh, God, she thought, her throat tightening. I've got to get out of this. Moving with extreme caution, she removed his arm, then began to ease herself away from him towards the edge of the bed. Only to feel him stir, and yawn, and come awake.

'Running out on me again, darling?' He reached for her, scooping her back into his embrace.

'What the hell do you think you're doing?' Paige tried furiously and unavailingly to free herself.

'I've been asleep,' he said. 'Why—do you own the franchise?'

'You said you'd use the chair,' she accused.

'I did,' he said. 'But it was so uncomfortable that chivalry lost out, I fear. Anyway, what's the problem? You didn't seem to object to my presence. In fact, you slept in my arms like a baby.'

'Well, I'm awake now,' Paige said curtly. 'And I'd like to get up, please.'

'What's the hurry?' Nick rested his chin on her shoulder. 'Minna may just be a memory, but there'll be a lot of cleaning up to do before the airport reopens. And there'll certainly be no planes out tonight. So why not relax and enjoy the facilities.'

'Let go of me.' Paige tried to pull free again. 'You have no right…'

'Take care, my sweet,' Nick said softly. 'You're on dangerous ground. Would you like us to discuss exactly what rights I do have where you're concerned?'

'You have none,' she flung back at him. 'Under the terms of our arrangement.'

He said slowly, 'An arrangement which made you my wife, Paige. Perhaps it's time you learned exactly what that means.'

'What are you talking about?' Her mouth was dry.

'I'm talking about our marriage.' His tone was almost matter of fact. 'I think it's time we forgot that damned agreement and made it a real one.'

Her voice shook. 'You said—no more games. You promised…'

'I said in future I'd be serious. Well, this is about as serious as it gets.'

'Never,' she said huskily. 'I'll never agree—and you can't make me.'

'I don't intend to use force, certainly. But persuasion's another matter entirely.' His lips gently grazed her neck. 'Don't you think?' He paused. 'After all, you wanted me once.'

What was she? she wondered wildly. Some toy to be picked up and discarded whenever the mood took him? She could have cried out with the hurt of it.

Instead, she filled her voice with ice. 'Please don't remind me. That was just a temporary aberration from which I've long since recovered.'

She felt him smile against her skin. 'Are you so sure of that?'

Inwardly she was trembling. But it was important vital—to at least appear in control.

She kept her voice cool. 'Twenty-four hours ago you were wrapped round some blonde. Take your powers of persuasion back to her, Nick. Because I don't think you're good husband material.'

'Why, darling,' he said mockingly, 'anyone would think you were jealous.'

'Then anyone would be wrong.' She paused. 'I'm just not interested in other women's leavings.'

She felt the sudden tension in the muscles that held her, and knew with a slight frisson of alarm that she had made him angry. He turned her in his arms to face him, his hands hard, pulling her roughly against his body.

He said, 'Try.' And his mouth took hers.

She intended to resist. To grant not even the least part of herself. But the pressure of his lips was too fierce, too compelling. Even as her hands braced against the wall of his chest in a vain attempt to push him away her lips were parting helplessly under his.

She tried to say no, but the word was swept away in the sweet savage flood of release that his kiss engendered.

She couldn't think, or breathe. She drank, unsated, from his mouth. His hand found her breast, moulded it through the clinging silk, his thumb stroking the hardening nipple.

And all the time the tearing, raging kiss went on.

Her heartbeat was going crazy, drumming a violent tattoo against her ribcage. The noise of it seemed to fill her ears, she thought dazedly—then realised in the same moment that it was someone knocking at the door of their room.

Nick lifted himself away from her, swearing savagely under his breath.

'What is it?' he called.

'From the management, sir.'

Nick swung himself off the bed and went over to the door. Paige seized the chance to get up too, seating herself in the despised chair while Nick spoke to the white-coated figure in the corridor.

'It seems they've managed to organise some hot food,' he said as he closed the door and turned back into the room. 'It's available in the dining room, if we want some.' His mouth twisted. 'I presume we do?'

'What kind of food?' Paige asked. She was astonished at the normality of her voice. 'I mean, is it lunch or dinner.'

Nick walked to the window and unfastened the bolts on the shutters, folding them back. Grey watery light seeped into the room. 'It's just gone six a.m. so I guess it's breakfast.'

Paige gasped. 'But it can't be. That would mean I'd been asleep for over twelve hours.'

He nodded. 'You were out for the count.'

She looked down at her hands, clenched together in her lap. 'I keep hoping I'm still asleep—and that all this is some horrible nightmare.'

He said softly, 'You're being provocative again, darling. Be thankful that my hunger for scrambled eggs temporarily outweighs my appetite for you.' He slid his wallet into the back pocket of his trousers. 'Are you coming down?'

'No, thank you.' Paige examined an imaginary fleck on her nail. 'I'm really not hungry at all.'

Nick shrugged. 'As you wish, darling. Stay here, instead, and rehearse being indifferent to me. You could certainly do with the practice,' he added mockingly from the doorway. 'And you can demonstrate your prowess when I return.'

For a moment his smile seemed to strip her naked, then the door closed behind him and Paige was alone.

She sat for a while, staring in front of her, her mind running in circles. Her lips felt tender, and her breasts ached in bittersweet arousal.

She couldn't believe how easily Nick had brought her to the edge of surrender, in spite of her high resolve. How could she have allowed him to kiss her—to touch her like that? she asked herself, shivering. As if she was some plaything for his pleasure. Why hadn't she fought—rejected him in her turn?

You fool, she castigated herself passionately. You weak, pathetic fool.

She got up, moving stiffly, and began to retrieve her belongings and thrust them into her bag.

When I return. His words seemed to hammer at her brain.

She felt the breath catch in her throat and her hands start to shake.

When he returned, she thought, she would not be here. She could not afford the risk.

She found the hotel information file in a drawer in the night table. She found the address of the consulate, copied it on to the back of the little town map, which was also included, and slipped it into her bag.

The lift wasn't working, of course, so she went down the stairs, half expecting to come face to face with Nick at any moment. But her luck held, and she was able to gain the ground floor in safety. Once there, the foyer was heaving with people, and it was comparatively simple to slide unobtrusively to the door. But with every step she took she was waiting to hear his voice calling her name, his hand on her shoulder.

Her heart was thudding like a steam hammer as she went outside. The wind was still quite fierce, but the air felt hot and dank. There was little traffic on the road, but people were scurrying about, heads bent, picking their way through the debris which littered the pavements.

Paige took a deep breath, hoisted her bag on to her shoulder, and began to run.

It was raining when she got back to the cottage. She put the car away and walked round to the front door, shoulders hunched in her thin jacket. It had been, she thought, the longest four days of her life.

The consulate staff had been kind, but harassed as they'd tried to deal with the problems of all the British nationals who'd been stranded. But when they'd discovered Paige wasn't hell-bent on obtaining a seat on the first plane out, they had happily found her a room with breakfast in a small, unpretentious hotel a couple of streets away. And there she had taken cover, only emerging when she'd been sure the backlog of passengers had been shifted and Nick was long gone.

The flight home had been dullness itself, and she'd slept through most of it.

Inside the hall, Paige paused for a moment, waiting for her home to work its usual magic and wrap unseen arms around her in comfort and welcome. But nothing happened. The air felt stale and chilly, the mat was littered with mail—mostly bills and circulars, by the look of it—and on the hall table the answering machine was blinking furiously.

Sighing, Paige put her travel bag by the stairs and pressed the button to retrieve her messages. They were all, she discovered without pleasure, from an increasingly agitated Toby. Something had clearly rattled his cage, and she was sure it wasn't simple concern for her well-being.

On the other hand there was no call from Nick, as she'd been half expecting, so maybe he still hadn't tracked her to her private hideaway—and that had to be a relief. Toby, she thought, her mouth twisting, she could deal with.

She went into the kitchen, filled the kettle and put it on the stove. She would go round to the Hall this evening, she decided. She'd called from Sainte Marie as soon as the phone service had been restored, to reassure her father that she was safe and well, but there were questions which needed to be asked—and answered—without delay.

She made her coffee and took it, with the pile of mail, into the sitting room. She went over to the casement to open a window, and as she did so heard a car come down the lane at speed and squeal to a halt at her gate.

A second later Toby strode grimly up the path and committed an assault on her brass door knocker. Mouth tightening, Paige went to admit him.

His opening was unpromising. 'Where the hell have you been?'

'Hello, brother dear, and it's good to see you too,' Paige returned with an affability she did not feel. 'Ever heard of Hurricane Minna?'

'That was ages ago,' he said impatiently. 'And you've been needed back here. I've got to talk to you.'

Paige groaned inwardly. 'I've only just arrived back,' she protested. 'Why don't I come over for dinner tonight, and we'll talk afterwards?'

He shook his head. 'It needs to be now, and in private.' He paused. 'We've got big trouble.'

'Really?' Paige shook her head. 'Well, I have problems of my own.' She paused. 'I—I ran into Nick Destry while I was away.'

'You did?' Toby stared at her. 'How did he seem? What did he say?'

Paige shrugged evasively. 'He was his usual obnoxious self.'

'Well, I hope to God you didn't upset him,' Toby said peevishly. 'Because we need him good-tempered and inclined to be generous. There's an emergency board meeting tomorrow, and all hell could break loose.'

Oh, no. The words groaned in her head. Paige swallowed. 'You'd better sit down,' she said bleakly. 'Do you want coffee?'

'I need a drink.' He glanced round. 'Scotch, if you've got it. And you'd better have one too.'

She walked to the corner cupboard, where she kept her small supply of alcohol, and splashed whisky into two tumblers.

She handed one to her brother. 'What's happened?'

He took a gulp of his drink. 'Remember the Seagrove development?'

'Of course,' she said. 'But that's finished, isn't it? All the houses were sold.'

He nodded. 'The first people were starting to move in

when they noticed cracks in the walls, and floors, and started complaining. We didn't take too much notice at first, because it's quite common in new houses as they settle. But they said it was worse than that, and got in their own independent surveyor to check.'

Toby shuddered. 'He had the foundations tested and said they were unsound. That there was too much sand and gravel in the soil, and the problem would just get worse and worse. He sent us this nightmare forty page report, and an estimate of how much it's going to cost to put right.' His voice sank to a whisper. 'Hundreds of thousands of pounds—and everyone will have to move out while the work is done, so there'll be compensation too.'

Paige stared at him, her lips parted in shock. 'But that's impossible.' Her voice was sharp. 'Presumably we had the soil tested. The lab's never let us down before.'

Toby stared down into his glass. 'We didn't use the normal lab,' he muttered. 'This guy I was at school with had just started up, and he was so much cheaper.'

'Did you consult your fellow directors about it?'

'I didn't think it was necessary,' he said defensively. 'He offered me this really good deal. I—I didn't see what could go wrong.'

Paige closed her eyes for a moment, and counted slowly to ten. Then, when she could trust her voice, 'Then we sue him.'

Toby shook his head miserably. 'He's gone into receivership. He owes the Revenue and the VAT, so we'd come a poor last even if he had any assets.' He stared at Paige with the eyes of a beaten dog. 'It's all down to Harrington Holdings. We're going to have to pay. And the residents are threatening to go to the press, as well as to court.'

Paige drew a deep breath. 'Do Maitland Destry know?'

'They didn't—at first. I thought I could maybe sort something out. But that accountant guy Nick installed to snoop on us got hold of the report and faxed it to him. So the balloon's gone up. He called this meeting three days ago—when he came back from vacation.'

'Yes,' she said quietly. 'Of course he did.'

There'd been no need to worry after all, she thought bleakly. Nick had more important matters to pursue than an errant wife.

'When you saw him, did he mention all this?'

'I suppose so,' Paige said wearily. 'But obliquely. I didn't really know what he was getting at.'

'Did he give any indication of what he might do? If he might be prepared to bail us out again?' There was a note of real desperation in Toby's voice. 'I tell you, Sis, if he resigns from the board, and Maitland Destry pull the rug out from under us, we're finished too. There's no way we can go on.'

'Do you think that's likely?' Paige traced the cut crystal of the tumbler with her forefinger. 'Surely he'll prefer to recoup his investment if he can?'

Toby shook his head. 'I just don't know any more. There are all kinds of rumours flying. Like he's going to bring in his own team to run the company. What will we do if that happens?'

Paige shrugged. 'Bite on the bullet and work with them, I suppose.'

'But that may not be an option.' He looked as if he was going to cry. 'People are saying we could all be sidelined, or worse. And who'd offer me another job once I'd been blacklisted by Nick Destry?'

She hesitated. 'Toby—I don't know what his plans are.'

'You must know something.' Toby faced her with sudden belligerence. 'You're his wife, for God's sake.'

'No.' Paige lifted her chin. 'And I never have been. It was only ever a paper marriage, as you know perfectly well.'

'So you say.' Toby hunched a petulant shoulder. 'But Denise is damned shrewd about these things, and she's always said you were both gagging for each other from day one.'

Paige's lip curled in distaste. 'Your wife has such a way with words. Besides, fooling her was part of the package, if you remember.'

'Well, try fooling your husband instead,' Toby said eagerly. 'You could get round him if you wanted—find out what he's planning. He's only a man, after all, so start behaving like a woman for once in your life.'

Paige set down her glass and rose. 'Let's pretend you didn't say that,' she told him quietly. 'I think you'd better go.'

Toby groaned. 'I'm sorry, Sis. I'm just at my wits' end. Clutching at straws.' He shook his head defeatedly as she accompanied him into the hall. 'You don't know what I've been through.'

Oh, don't I? Paige asked herself silently, watching Toby walk back to his car with an air of despondency that was almost tangible.

She lay back in her chair, closing her eyes, her body slumped wearily against the cushions as she reviewed what Nick had said regarding company business in the time she'd spent with him.

I should have listened more closely, she thought. Asked more questions. But I had more pressing things on my mind.

Looking back, it was clear Nick had expected her to know about the Seagrove fiasco. Yet instinct told her that wasn't all of it. That other things were about to come out of the woodwork. And Toby's flakiness only served to reinforce this suspicion.

What the *hell* had been going on?

She sighed. Well, tomorrow everything would become

brutally clear. And she would have to stand shoulder to shoulder with her family and fight Nick in a battle they might not win.

She'd thought she'd been so clever when she left him at the hotel. But Nick had probably anticipated precisely that. Even allowed it to happen, because he knew that eventually there would be nowhere for her to run. That she would have to face him in some personal Armageddon of his own engineering.

Because he would make it personal. She knew it in every fibre of her being. Tomorrow's fight would be between the two of them. And his terms were already on the table.

A small, uncontrollable shiver ran through her.

She sat up abruptly. Sitting here brooding was useless, she told herself forcefully. She would unpack, and relax in a hot bath for a while before she made herself some supper. Then an early night seemed sensible. After all, she needed to be rested and strong for the meeting. *For the battle.*

She picked up her cold coffee and carried it into the kitchen. Later she'd brew herself some herb tea, she decided, emptying the beaker down the sink. Do all the normal, familiar things. Start drawing her life back around her like a security blanket.

As she went back into the hall to retrieve her bag the sound of the front door knocker echoed through the cottage.

Paige groaned inwardly. Toby again, she supposed without pleasure. Passing on more bad news or exercising his powers of persuasion—and both equally unacceptable.

She walked unsmilingly to the door and threw it wide, already rehearsing the words of dismissal. And stopped, her eyes widening in shock and incredulity.

'So you're safely home,' Nick said softly. 'And now, perhaps, we can have that long overdue conversation. Just the two of us.'

CHAPTER NINE

SHE said hoarsely, 'What are you doing here? How did you find me?'

His brows lifted. 'It's hardly a state secret. Your whereabouts are well documented in the office files.'

Her fingers tightened on the edge of the door. 'But you never came here before.'

His faint grin was wry. 'Perhaps I doubted my welcome. Even now it's hardly overwhelming.' There was rain glistening on his hair and shoulders. 'May I come in?'

She hesitated perceptibly, then stood aside, allowing him to enter the hall. She said tautly, 'Please say what you have to say, then go.'

He tutted reprovingly. 'I'm sure your family would prefer you to be more hospitable than this, darling. Is that the sitting room?'

He walked past her and stood for a moment, surveying the pale walls and low-beamed ceiling, the seagrass flooring and the two deeply cushioned sofas upholstered in dark blue which faced each other from either side of the stone fireplace with its dog grate.

He said expressionlessly, 'Very charming.'

'Please don't patronise me,' Paige said stonily. 'I'm well aware that the whole cottage would fit into a corner of your London house.' *And you make it seem smaller simply by being here.*

'You've never been to my London house.'

'I've seen pictures of it.' Paige cursed herself inwardly for that little piece of self-betrayal.

'Well,' he said softly, 'perhaps you'll get to know it a

little more intimately in the near future.' He paused. 'Are you going to ask me to sit down?'

'If I must.'

He said gently, 'Let's get one thing straight, sweetheart. You're not going to drive me away by behaving like a stroppy little cat. Now, ask me nicely.'

Paige bit her lip. 'Please—take a seat.'

'Thank you,' he said politely, and went to the furthest sofa. He was wearing the usual City gear of dark suit, pristine white shirt and elegant silk tie. He looked cool and in control, and she felt like a physical and mental wreck. She stood watching him, her face set rigidly. Waiting for what was to come.

He looked at the low rosewood table which occupied the space between the sofas and his brows lifted.

'Dutch courage, Mrs Destry?'

'I wasn't aware I needed it.'

He sighed, 'Paige, there are two glasses, and I'll lay money that the empty one belongs to your brother. I imagine he's filled you in on everything that's been happening while you've been disporting yourself in the Caribbean, so you know that all the news is bad.' He shrugged. 'Unless you've drunk both whiskies yourself, making me just another discredited conspiracy theorist.'

'A visit from Toby is hardly a conspiracy,' Paige said coldly. 'And, yes, he thought I should know about the Seagrove problem, as the press will have to be dealt with. I'll draft a statement for approval at tomorrow's meeting.'

'It's a kind thought,' he said. 'But Craddock Peters PR will be handling the media for Harringtons from now on. You can bring your resignation letter to the meeting instead.'

She gasped. 'You're—firing me? But you can't. The rest of the board would never agree. My father persuaded me to take the job in the first place.'

'And a very cosy little arrangement it's been.' Nick's tone held a sudden harshness. 'Only it's over, and I strongly advise you not to make a fuss or sue for unfair dismissal. Let's not wash any more Harrington dirty linen in public.'

'Dirty linen—are you crazy?' Paige shook her head. 'Is this some kind of punishment for being on vacation when the Seagrove thing blew up? Because I'll have you know it was my first holiday in two years.'

'You seem to be forgetting,' he said gently, 'the few days we shared in Normandy.'

'I haven't forgotten a thing.'

'I don't actually care how many holidays you fit into your year,' he went on, as if she hadn't spoken. 'As long as you pay for them yourself out of your over-inflated salary and don't fiddle them as a company expense. As you also charge the mortgage on this little *pied-à-terre,* incidentally,' he added grimly. 'And your furnishing and decorating bills.'

If he'd lifted his arm and struck her to the floor she could not have been more shocked. Or bewildered. Or seethingly angry.

Her fists clenched involuntarily at her sides as words of furious denial began to form in her brain. She was earning only two-thirds of her previous salary at Harringtons, and the mortgage ate a big chunk of it. She'd painted the cottage herself at weekends, and bought the main pieces of furniture out of her savings—although her father had given her a few items from the Hall too.

And but for Angie's generosity, she thought wildly, she'd never have gone anywhere near the Caribbean.

And so she would tell him, at the top of her voice, with no expletives deleted.

Except...

Suddenly the burning, strident anger bubbling to her lips was giving way to concern—even fear. And the voice in her head was telling her to slow down and proceed with caution, because there was something terribly wrong here.

She moved stiffly to the other sofa and sat down. She said, 'How did you discover—all this?'

'The credit goes to my accountant, Jake Allenby. I don't think he relished having to tell me that my wife was using the company as her own private piggy bank, but he did it anyway. He's going to be heading a team investigating other more serious discrepancies as well.'

'What sort of—discrepancies?'

'You mean you don't know?' he derided. 'The Harrington name for quality and integrity has been taking quite a beating lately. People have paid for top-of-the-range kitchens and bathrooms and had cheap imitations installed instead. On one site the central heating specifications were changed, which led to potentially dangerous fumes entering the houses. Elsewhere various inclusive items like landscaping and car ports have been charged as extras. Thieving has reached epidemic proportions right across the board. Need I go on?'

She kept her voice steady while her mind worked frantically. 'And you're holding me responsible for all this?'

He said wearily, 'Don't be absurd. But it's all part of a general attitude that cheating's fine and the company and its clients simply exist to be ripped off. And for the company also read Maitland Destry.' He shook his head. 'It can't go on, Paige. I won't allow it. And you're the first casualty.'

All that money, she thought, being claimed each month on her behalf. But not by her. So who could it be?

A chilling image of Toby, here in this room only half an hour before, hangdog and panicking, rose in her mind. Toby—always short of cash to fund Denise's latest extravagances.

Oh, no, she thought, swallowing back nausea. Dear God—no.

She picked up her whisky. Drank some to give herself a breathing space. Thinking time. And to dispel the ice clamped round her heart.

Nick was watching her, his eyes narrowed. He said, 'What's the matter, Paige. Did you think you wouldn't be found out?'

She said quietly, 'I don't really know what I thought.' She drew a deep breath, then forced herself to meet his gaze. 'I'll start looking for another job tomorrow. I still have contacts.' She paused. 'And if you promise not to take your investigations into this any further, I'll pay you back every penny out of my future salary.'

'Yes,' Nick said softly. 'It is indeed payback time. But there's no need for you to go job-hunting because you already have a post waiting for you. As my wife. Starting at once. And this time there'll be no excuses, or evasions, or running away.'

She'd been expecting it—dreading it. And now it was upon her.

'Please.' She looked at him pleadingly, desperation in her voice. 'You can't do this. It's—obscene. Medieval. Punish me in some other way, but not this.'

'You're hardly flattering, darling,' Nick drawled. 'But it won't be so bad. I can't allow you unlimited access to my money, of course, but you'll be paid an allowance, and all your bills will be sent to me.' He paused, the dark eyes scanning her. 'I'm prepared to be generous, Paige, but I expect my money's worth, too. You won't short-change me in bed.'

Her whole body winced. She thought of his hands touching her—his mouth—exacting his own dark retribution for her supposed sins. And somehow she would have to bear it. Because it was better for Nick to blame her than discover the real truth.

Toby was weak and a fool, and what he'd done was probably criminal too, but she couldn't bear to see him publicly disgraced as he was bound to be—not for his own sake, but her father's. The shock might trigger off another heart attack—and this one could be fatal.

On the other hand she couldn't just passively accept the fate Nick had condemned her to either.

She said huskily, 'Nick—we'll only make each other wretched like this, and you know it. If you'll let me go, I'll work like a demon to repay the money. I swear it. And we can both be free to find happiness—properly.' She bit her lip. 'After all, there's your blonde.'

'Ah, yes,' he said softly. 'The gorgeous Michelle. She really needled you, didn't she, darling? I wonder why.'

She said sharply, 'You were practically wearing her—' and stopped, cursing herself under her breath.

'And how do you categorise your own cavortings with Brad Coulter?' There was sudden danger in his voice.

'Why, Nick.' It was her turn to mock. 'Don't tell me you were jealous.'

'Hardly.' He shrugged, his mouth hardening. 'After all, I left you free to roam. I can't really repine if you used that freedom to let some stud charm you into bed. But even if we divorced there's no guarantee that Coulter would ever marry you. He prefers less formal arrangements, by all accounts.'

Paige lifted her chin. 'Clearly you both have so much in common.'

He said lightly, 'Then you'll be able to compare notes, won't you, darling?'

She bent her head. 'Is this discussion over now?' she asked flatly. 'Because, if so, I'd rather like to be alone. I have a lot to think about.'

'Then I'm sorry to disappoint you,' he said, 'but I'm not leaving. Our marriage begins here and now—tonight.'

'But that's not possible.' She looked at him imploringly. 'I—I need time.'

'And I have needs, too,' he said. 'Rather more basic, but equally urgent, I promise you.' He got to his feet. 'Where are your keys?'

'Why do you want them?' Her brain seemed to be in meltdown. Nothing made sense any more.

'I have some things to bring in from the car.' He smiled at her. 'And I would hate to find myself locked out and be forced to call in one of the Harrington carpenters to take the door off its hinges. I'm sure you wouldn't care for it either,' he added gently.

'No,' Paige said, and swallowed. 'They—they're on the hall table.'

'Very wise,' he said. 'I won't be long.'

She sat, huddled into the corner of the sofa, staring blindly into space. How could she do this? How could she yield herself to the demands of this totally cynical arrangement? Give herself to a man who neither loved nor respected her? Who actually thought she was some kind of minor embezzler—a freeloader of the worst kind?

Toby had asked her to use her influence, she recalled painfully, and she'd refused, secure in her position on the moral high ground. Now the earth was shaking under her, and all her certainties were gone.

The misdemeanours she was being blamed for were relatively minor compared with the others that Nick had mentioned. Those that were still being investigated.

Sick instinct warned her that Toby was probably involved up to his neck, and that next time she might not be able to save him. But she still had to try, she thought, a wave of desolation sweeping over her. Whatever the cost.

She heard Nick return, and straightened her shoulders instinctively.

'Do I get the guided tour?' He stood in the doorway, suitcase in hand. 'Or must I find my own way?'

'It's the door to the right at the top of the stairs.' She steadied her voice. Made it almost businesslike. 'The bathroom's opposite, and you'll find spare towels in the airing cupboard.'

In a moment, she thought, astonished, I'll be offering him a wake-up call and asking if he wants to order a newspaper.

He nodded, unfazed. 'There's a hamper of food in the kitchen. You might want to unpack it.'

'Food?' Paige echoed in disbelief.

'Of course. Second rule of marriage, darling. Regular meals.' He gave her a mocking grin. 'Want to know what the first rule is?'

'I can guess,' she said shortly. 'But I'll get you something to eat, if that's what you want.'

'It will do,' he said. 'To begin with.' And a moment later she heard him going up the stairs.

It was a large hamper, bearing the label of a famous London shop. Investigating the contents, Paige found a cold roasted duck, various salads, bread, cheese, a wonderful *tarte tatin* and a bottle of good claret. In a separate container she discovered smoked bacon and half a dozen free-range eggs.

For the man who plans to stay for breakfast, she thought, biting her lip.

She set the food out on to plates, and was shocked to find her mouth watering. She'd originally planned to set just one place at the table in her tiny dining room, but the aroma of the duck was too appealing for pride. And besides, starving herself would solve nothing.

She used her favourite embroidered linen placemats with

the best silver and crystal and tall candles in elegant wooden holders. She put the duck on a carving platter and uncorked the wine to let it breathe.

She was in the kitchen, making her own dressing for the salad, when she heard Nick descend the stairs. Earlier she'd heard the water running, and guessed he was having a bath.

She'd planned to do that, she thought, back in some other lifetime, when her most serious problem had been a difficult board meeting in the morning.

He'd changed into cream chinos and a casual black polo shirt, she saw in the swift sideways glance which was all she allowed herself.

'It all looks wonderful.' He propped himself in the doorway. How could he seem so much at ease when she was like a coiled spring? Paige wondered desperately, feeling the drag of his attraction curling through her like a seventh wave. 'Impressing me with your hostess skills, darling?'

She shrugged. 'I enjoy entertaining,' she returned coolly. 'Although I prefer to choose my own guests.'

'And make sure that they're just passing through?' He waited for her reluctant nod, his mouth twisting. 'But I'm here to stay, Paige,' he told her softly. 'And the sooner you accustom yourself to that, the better.' He paused. 'Do you understand?'

'Yes—yes, I understand.' Paige concentrated her attention fiercely on the amount of wine vinegar she was adding to the fragrant green-gold olive oil in an attempt to subdue her fierce awareness of him.

And he'd seen her bedroom. He'd been in there, hanging his clothes in her wardrobe. Making room among her things for his own.

No doubt she could now expect some loaded comment about the fact that she'd been sleeping alone in a double bed.

Instead, he said quietly, 'Can I get you a drink?'

More Dutch courage? she thought. Or anaesthetic?

She said, like a polite child, 'Thank you—no.'

He stayed where he was, watching her. 'It feels damp, and a bit chilly tonight,' he went on. 'Would you like me to light the fire in the sitting room?'

It was only what she'd intended to do herself, but she heard herself saying waspishly, 'Please—make yourself at home.'

He smiled at her. 'Thank you. I have every intention of doing so.'

He vanished, and presently she heard the murmur of the television.

The fact that he was here, in the cottage, invading her own private space and making it his, somehow made the whole bad situation even worse, Paige thought as she coated the salad leaves with dressing and carried the bowl to the dining room.

Nick responded immediately to her stilted announcement that the meal was ready.

'I wanted us to have another picnic, but the weather's too foul, so this seemed the next best thing,' he said as he carved the duck. He slanted a swift smile at her. 'Remember our day on the beach at Les Sables d'Or?'

'Not really,' Paige denied defensively.

He clicked his tongue reprovingly. 'You shouldn't fib, darling. Your eyes change colour—become much darker.'

She stifled a small gasp. 'They do nothing of the kind.'

'How would you know?' Nick handed her a plate. 'Have a look in a mirror next time you're inclined to be economical with the *actualité* and you'll see what I mean.'

Paige gave him a mutinous look and helped herself to new potatoes in a mayonnaise and chive dressing.

'Maybe we should have a toast.' He poured the deep red wine into her glass. 'Can you suggest something appropriate?'

Paige shrugged. 'Cheers?' she offered coldly.

'I don't think so.' He lifted his glass, and unwillingly she followed suit. 'Here's to life—and not being afraid of the dark.'

She felt her face warm, and took a hasty sip of the wine with an incoherent murmur. Why, she thought, did he have to remind her of those traumatic moments—and what they'd led to?

It was a largely silent meal. Paige searched desperately but vainly for some innocuous topic of conversation, and Nick seemed preoccupied with his own thoughts.

Perhaps this was what married couples did, she thought as she served the *tarte tatin*.

When they'd finished eating, Nick helped her clear the table.

'No dishwasher?' he asked, brows raised as Paige ran hot water into the sink and added washing up liquid.

She sent him a defiant glance. 'I considered it, but decided not to push my luck.' *Or my savings account.*

He gave her a meditative look. 'Can I help put things away?'

'No, thanks. This kitchen isn't really big enough for two.'

And neither is this house, a voice inside her cried out wildly. Or this universe.

He looked at her for another long moment, then turned away without further comment.

She left the dishes to drain, then found a fresh packet of rich Colombian blend and filled the cafetière.

Nick was lounging on one of the sofas watching television when she carried in the tray and set it on the rosewood table. But as she moved to sit opposite him he reached out an imperative hand.

'No.' His voice was quiet, but very definite. 'Come here.'

She swallowed nervously, then obeyed, sinking into the

soft cushion beside him. He put an arm round her shoulders, drawing her against him.

'Relax,' he suggested softly. 'You're so brittle you could break.'

'I can't deal with this,' Paige whispered. She shook her head. 'I don't know what to do.'

'You have to sit with me and watch a wildlife documentary.' There was faint amusement in his voice. 'That's not so difficult.'

'That,' she said, 'isn't what I mean.'

'No,' he said. 'But it's enough for now.'

His hand moved on her shoulder and arm, stroking them gently, rhythmically—as if, Paige thought, she was a nervous animal he had to soothe. And, oddly, it was calming. Her heartbeat had slowed to a normal level and the iron band gripping her throat had gone too.

The rain was lashing against the window, but inside the room was golden in the crackling firelight. As if we were caught in amber, Paige thought dreamily.

Even when she moved to pour their coffee it seemed natural, even essential, to return to his embrace afterwards, settling against the curve of his lean body as if she belonged there.

She thought, 'I don't understand,' and realised when she felt him smile against her hair that she'd spoken the thought aloud.

'We're having a quiet evening at home,' he told her quietly. 'Probably just as you'd planned to do on your own.'

She said without thinking, 'Actually, I was going to have a bath and an early night,' and could have bitten out her tongue.

'That,' he said softly, taking her coffee cup and putting it back on the table, 'is an even better plan.' He smiled down into her startled eyes. 'Don't you agree?'

She'd told him she needed more time, but what she really

needed was his mouth on hers, she realised as his free hand cupped her face, tilting it upwards for his kiss.

His lips were warm and seductively gentle as they parted hers. His fingers caressed the nape of her neck and the vulnerable curve of her throat, and her whole body sighed with pleasure.

He was lighting slow fires in her veins. She could feel her breathing quicken, and stars dance behind her closed and heavy eyelids.

She moved closer to him, pressing herself against him, feeling the tips of her breasts graze his chest as the dark witchery of sexual desire began to awaken inside her.

They clung together, their mouths aching and burning in an ever-increasing hunger.

When at last he lifted his head, Paige stared up at him with dazed eyes.

He touched her face with light fingers—her cheekbones, her reddened mouth. Then he got to his feet, pulling her up after him.

He said softly, 'It's time you went to bed, Mrs Destry.'

And she went with him, hand in hand, up the stairs into the friendly darkness.

At the door, he halted. 'I'll run your bath for you.' He hesitated. 'And there's something I should tell you. I've decided to sleep in the spare room tonight, after all.'

Her eyes searched his face incredulously, disappointment twisting like a claw inside her. 'But why?' She bit her lip, forcing out the reluctant words. 'Don't—don't you want me?'

'Yes,' he said with sudden harshness. 'I want you. But that isn't the point. I realised earlier that this isn't the ideal time for us.' He shook his head. 'There's too much background stuff—too many unanswered questions hanging over us. Besides, you were right. You do need time. Time to get used to the idea of having me around. And I—I'm not sure I'm capable tonight of being as patient as you deserve.'

He drew a deep breath. 'Believe me, it's better this way.' He dropped a swift, rough kiss on her hair. 'Now have your bath and get some rest. Tomorrow's going to be a tough day.'

She went slowly into her bedroom and closed the door. In the lamplight the big bed with its single pillow arranged chastely in the middle seemed to be mocking her.

But tonight there was something else on the bed as well. A square flat box, striped in blue and silver with long silver ribbons, was lying on the coverlet.

She sat on the edge of the bed, and pulled the box towards her. She untied the ribbons, lifted the lid, and parted the folds of tissue. It was a nightgown, she realised, white chiffon layered over silk, the narrow straps made of silk flowers and the same decoration edging the demure bodice. A filmy, exquisite thing. And the accompanying card said simply, 'From Nick.'

It was beautiful, she thought. And it was for her. She sat holding it, waiting until she heard Nick come out of the bathroom, walk along the passage to the spare room and close the door. And then she got to her feet, her mind made up.

There were scented candles on the wide ledge round the bath, and he'd lit them. The water was perfumed too, and foaming gently as Paige slid into it. Letting the bubbles drift over her body, she turned her head slightly and looked at the nightdress spread across a chair, feeling the tingle of anticipation—of excitement in her senses.

She dried herself on a bath sheet and applied body lotion in her favourite scent to her skin. She brushed her hair until it shone, then slipped the gown over her head, and fastened the one tiny silk-covered button at the back of the bodice.

She studied herself for a moment in the long mirror. It wasn't overtly sexy. It wasn't even particularly revealing. But it was beautiful—and right. So right.

All she needed now was courage—and a little bit of luck.

A sliver of light showed under Nick's door. She turned the handle and went in. He was lying propped up on one elbow, reading. His skin looked dramatically dark against the white linen sheets, and she felt a surge of longing for him, potent as an electrical charge.

His head came up sharply and he stared at her, frowning a little.

'What is it, Paige?'

'I came to show you your present.' She turned slowly in a circle. 'And to thank you. It's the loveliest nightgown I ever possessed. The loveliest gift I ever received, too.'

'I'm glad you like it.' He sounded far too cool and controlled. 'I thought…' He stopped abruptly, and hope rose within her.

'What did you think?'

He said slowly, 'I suppose—that every girl has the right to look like a bride—on her wedding night.'

'Is it my wedding night, Nick?' Her low voice trembled a little. 'Then why do I have to sleep alone?'

'I explained all that.'

'I know. But I don't have to accept your explanation.' She took a step nearer to the bed. 'You see, I want you near me, and I'm not sure I can be patient either.'

He groaned. 'Paige—don't do this to me. I've done nothing but screw up since the first day I saw you. Let me try and do the right thing for once.'

'There's only one right thing,' she said. 'And that's for us to be together tonight.'

She knew exactly how she looked. Her hair a gleaming

cloud. Her eyes heavy with the desire she no longer had to pretend did not exist. Her mouth still faintly swollen from his kisses. And her skin like a pearl against the drift of chiffon.

'But this bed's too small,' she added. 'We'd be more comfortable in mine. Bring another pillow with you.'

She turned away and walked to the door. She didn't look back. To do so would have been a sign of weakness, she told herself. A lapse in confidence.

Because he would follow her. She was sure of it.

She went into her own room and stood by the bed. She reached for her pillow and moved it to one side. Making room for him. The hammer of her heart was almost deafening in the stillness.

Nick came in, wearing his silk robe. He tossed his pillow on to the bed and looked at her searchingly. He said, 'Am I the first?'

Faint colour stained her face. 'Does it matter?'

'You know it does.' His voice was grave. 'I want to make it good for you, Paige, and that could mean I need to retain a measure of control. So answer me, please.'

'Yes,' she said with sudden passion. 'You're the first. Of course you are. How could there be anyone else?'

He bent his head in acknowledgement. 'I don't deserve it.' He paused. 'Are you absolutely sure about this—because it's not too late…'

'It's always been too late.' She reached behind her and released the button from its clasp. She slid the straps down from her shoulders. The loosened gown whispered its way to the floor, pooling round her feet.

For a moment she was still in the lamplight, letting his eyes feast on her. Then she turned back the covers and slipped into the bed. She lifted her hands to push back her hair, her rounded breasts tilting deliciously.

Then she smiled at him. She said, 'I've waited a year, Nick. Isn't that enough?'

'More than enough,' he assented huskily. He took off his robe and threw it aside, making no attempt to hide that he was starkly, powerfully aroused.

He joined her, reaching across the bed for her with a hunger that consumed them both.

Their mouths clung, scalding, scorching. His hands stroked her skin, making her shiver with delight. His fingers encompassed her breasts, caressing her nipples to a fever-pitch of sensitivity.

She turned restlessly in his arms, offering herself with a frantic completeness, her words echoing his exploration of her, paying homage to his strength and potency, forcing him to groan his pleasure in turn.

He began to kiss her body, his lips reverent, as if every inch of her skin was precious to him, making her senses leap and sing. Her pulses were going crazy, the blood turning to honey in her veins.

His hands grazed her flanks, then moved to her thighs, and she gasped at the intimate brush of his fingers, the rush of moist heat his touch engendered.

He knew so well how to touch—and where, she thought, her mind reeling. He found the tiny peak of secret flesh, teasing it exquisitely, making her writhe and moan until he silenced her gently with his lips.

A strange, breathless tension was building inside her. She was straining, reaching for something that remained tantalisingly beyond her grasp.

Nick moved over her—above her—and she felt the heat and strength of him touching her, and sobbed her need and acceptance against his mouth.

'I don't want to hurt you.' His voice was hoarse—a stranger's. It reached her from the far distance.

But how could it hurt when this was what she craved?

'Anything.' Her small breathless croak was almost unrecognisable. 'Anything. Just—don't stop.'

Her urgent fingers cupped him, explored and stroked and cherished. Then welcomed him to the warmth of her threshold and beyond.

He took her slowly, gentling his way with infinite care into her body until his possession was complete, his whole being alert to every tiny nuance of response from her.

But she was ready—so ready. And when, at last, she held him within her, she moaned her pleasure aloud.

Her fingers gripped his shoulders and her slender legs clamped around his lean hips as he began to move, slowly at first, then more strongly, drawing her with him into the ancient rhythm of passion. Gasping, she rose and fell on a tide of mounting sensation, all control gone, her body striving blindly for a culmination she could only guess at.

And when it came at last it overwhelmed her. From one tiny pinpoint of pleasure and release, a thousand ripples, seemed to spread—until her whole body pulsated in an agony of rapture.

And as she fell, spiralling through some exquisite void, crying out his name, there were tears on her face. And his.

CHAPTER TEN

PAIGE lay in Nick's arms, mindless, boneless, her smile kissing his sweat-slicked shoulder.

'I didn't know.' Her voice was small, breathless. 'I never dreamed…'

His arm tightened round her. 'I always did,' he murmured. 'From that first moment in the wine bar I realised how it would be.'

'Oh, God.' A tremor of laughter shook her. 'Now, I die a thousand deaths each time I remember that.'

'Then don't. You mustn't blame fate for the way it brought us together.' He was silent for a moment. 'I went after you when you left. I'd been a bastard to you, and it was totally unnecessary—a complete overreaction to being suddenly confronted by the only woman I'd ever want. I was terrified I'd blown the whole thing, particularly as you disappeared.'

'I'll say I did,' Paige said devoutly. 'I just wanted to distance myself completely.'

'But one of the guys I was with knew you,' Nick went on, dropping a kiss on her hair. 'He said you were "the Harrington girl" but you weren't involved in the company—and just as well, because it was in deep trouble and looking for outside investment. But no one would touch them because the board was family only. And who was going to advance that kind of money without a measure of serious control?

'And that, of course, made me think. Quite apart from enabling me to see you again, it seemed to me that Harringtons was worth rescuing. It occurred to me that if I was prepared to restore their good name you might be grateful. Even grateful enough to marry me.'

He sighed. 'But I soon realised I was involved in a full-scale financial emergency and there was going to be no time for the kind of leisurely wooing I'd had in mind. Besides, I was terrified that someone else might appear waving a chequebook and your brother would marry you off to him instead.'

'Do you think I'd have agreed?' Paige was horrified.

'How was I to know? Our preliminary encounters hadn't been exactly promising. And I'd already discovered you were devoted to your father. Maybe you'd have preferred any alternative to me.' He grimaced. 'I decided the best plan was a pre-emptive strike. So I offered the only kind of deal I thought you might just accept.'

'And if I hadn't?'

'Then I'd have reverted to Plan B—the flowers, the phone calls, the champagne dinners. I kept remembering the chemistry there'd been between us for that first minute in the wine bar. The way I couldn't believe my luck when you walked towards me. I told myself that somehow I'd find that spark again.'

'You were very sure of yourself.' Paige bit his shoulder gently.

'Not at all,' he denied instantly. 'I rushed you into the wedding because I was so scared that you'd take fright and pull out of the whole thing.' He shook his head. 'I wanted you desperately, but you seemed encased in ice whenever I was around. And I'd put myself in this trap by promising that it was going to be a business relationship only. It wasn't until I broke all the rules and kissed you that I thought there might be hope.'

Paige lifted herself on to an elbow and looked down at him, smoothing the damp dark hair back from his forehead.

'Taking me on honeymoon was hardly within the terms of the contract either,' she pointed out.

'No, but when Grandmère offered the house it seemed a chance for us to spend some time together without outside interference, as well as convince any snoopers that it was a real marriage. I thought—If I can just get her on my side, that will be a start.'

'And getting me into that enormous bed?' Her brows lifted quizzically.

He grinned lazily up at her. 'That,' he said, 'would have been a bonus.'

She was silent for a moment. Then she said with difficulty, 'Then why did you walk away that night? When you must have known I wanted you, too?'

'Yes,' he said quietly. 'I knew—and it was the worst kind of hell. Because I realised that seducing you—persuading you to enjoy sex with me—was only a small part of what I really wanted. Watching you play with that baby on the beach was like a revelation. It made me understand that only a complete relationship, with all that implied, would do for me.

'But there was no guarantee you felt the same. You needed me at that moment because you were scared of the dark, but you might have felt very differently in daylight. And I couldn't handle a one-night stand—not with my lady, the woman I loved.'

'Why didn't you say something...?'

'In case I didn't get the answer I wanted.' His mouth twisted wryly. 'So I chickened out, and regretted it ever after. I was over the moon when you took the PR job with Harringtons,' he added wryly. 'Because I thought it meant I'd see you on a regular basis—start making amends.' He shook his head. 'But how wrong I was. I realised at once you were deliberately avoiding me, and I felt like a leper. I told myself that it was hopeless. That it might even be better to let you have the divorce and then ask if we could start again somehow. But when I saw you on St Antoine with Brad Coulter I knew there was no way I was going to let you go.'

Paige bit her lip. 'You weren't on your own either that night.'

'No,' he said. 'I was with Alain Froyat's daughter, a very young, hideously spoiled rich bitch who'd decided to use me to make her boyfriend jealous. And as Alain's a client I could hardly give Michelle the tongue-lashing she so richly deserved.'

Paige's lips quivered into a smile. 'Did it work with the boyfriend? Because it certainly did for me.' She paused, choosing her words carefully. 'But then I'd had plenty of time to be jealous. You'd hardly been leading the life of a hermit while we were apart.'

'I certainly put on a good act,' Nick agreed. 'Enough to keep the gossip columns ticking over.'

'Was that all it was?' she queried unhappily. 'Gossip?'

'I lead a high-profile life, my love. You didn't want to be with me, and I wasn't going to wear my heart on my sleeve. So I was seen with a lot of women. But when the evening ended I went home alone. I always hoped that one day, by some miracle, I'd win you over, and I wasn't going to let anyone or anything jeopardise that.'

'I could hardly pick up a paper without seeing some picture of you with another girl.' Paige bit her lip. 'I told myself I didn't care, and that it would just make the divorce easier, but underneath I was hurting so badly. I used to wake up in the night crying, glad I couldn't remember my dreams.'

'I would never have guessed. When I talked to you on the beach that night your indifference was like a brick wall,' he said ruefully. 'But then I wasn't thinking particularly straight. Jake Allenby, who was riding shotgun on

Harringtons for me, was sending me daily doses of information that I didn't want to hear. There was cheating going on all through the organisation—and the biggest cheat of all, it seemed, was my marriage.

'I decided there and then that was all going to change,' he added with a touch of grimness. 'That you'd been getting away with it in every way for too long and I was going to put a stop to it. When we were stranded by the hurricane I finally had the chance to be alone with you—talk things out. But I still couldn't get near you.' He paused. 'Until the power went off. And then you were suddenly vulnerable again, like that night in France—and as much out of my reach for all the same reasons.'

He looked up at her, his face grave. 'Why are you afraid of the dark, Paige? I've always wondered.'

'It's just a stupid thing.' She bit her lip. 'Someone told me when I was little that monsters hid in your room, in the cupboards and under the beds, and after that I always had a nightlight. Then my mother went down with appendicitis, and I was sent to stay with a schoolfriend's family. They had a nanny who didn't believe in indulging children with bedroom lights, and she took it away with her. I woke up and found myself in a strange room—and suddenly the monsters were right there with me. I started screaming and couldn't stop.

'I think my friend's parents decided I was unbalanced,' she added ruefully. 'They were kind at the time, but I was never asked to stay with Belinda again, and the following term she found another best friend. I always thought I'd grow out of it, but I never have.'

He stroked her cheek with a gentle hand. 'Don't be so sure of that. I'm here now.' He paused. 'And I don't need to ask who scared you in the first place. Your bloody brother has a lot to answer for.'

'All younger sisters get teased. It's an occupational hazard.' She shrugged a bare shoulder. 'He wasn't to know I was such a wimp.'

'I don't think he knows much about you at all.' The dark eyes narrowed slightly. 'Was he aware that you were using the company as a neighbourhood cashpoint, for instance?'

Paige's throat tightened suddenly. Oh, God, she thought. How easily being happy had made her forget the financial mess that Toby had created for her. But she couldn't let herself forget. Nick might be prepared to forgive her, but her brother was a different matter entirely.

I can never let him find out, she thought with a pang.

And surely taking the blame for Toby's sins was a small price to pay for the bright promise of the future.

She didn't look at him. 'He—never mentioned it.' She hesitated. 'I'm sorry. So sorry for everything.' She drew a breath. 'I—I can't believe you still want to be with me.'

'As much as I need to go on breathing.' He pulled her down to him and kissed her, his lips moving on hers with infinite tenderness. 'But you understand there'll have to be changes.'

'Does anyone else know why I'm leaving Harringtons?' she asked haltingly.

'Only Jake,' he said. 'And he works strictly for me.'

'In a way, it will be a relief.' That at least was the truth. 'I never really wanted the job.'

'Next you'll be telling me it was all a subconscious desire to be fired,' Nick said drily.

'Or a devious way of attracting your attention?' she mused.

'You always had that,' he said. 'You weren't the only one who found it hard to sleep at night.' He turned to glance at her little bedside clock. 'But now, my love, maybe we should do exactly that.'

'You think so?' She allowed her hand to stray delicately, but with provocation. 'I had other plans.'

Nick firmly captured her fingers. 'Behave. You're still a bit too new to all this, and fragile, for a repeat performance.'

Paige moved closer, moving her hips sensuously against his.

'Are you quite sure about that?' she whispered, her smile catlike as she experienced his immediate and involuntary reaction.

Groaning, Nick tipped up her face and kissed her hungrily.

'Then don't say you weren't warned,' he muttered against her lips. 'Because this is only the beginning.

She awoke slowly and luxuriously, stretching her body experimentally. Yes, she ached a little, but it was more than worth it, she thought, remembering in vivid and glorious detail the intensity and passion with which Nick had pleasured her.

The bed beside her was empty, however, and when she looked at the clock she realised why.

Good God. She threw the covers aside. The board meeting. Why on earth didn't Nick wake me?

Obviously he'd thought she'd be too embarrassed to hand in her resignation in person and was trying to spare her, she realised with a pang. But she needed to be there to warn Toby that Nick had discovered his expenses scam and tell him that she was covering up for him.

She grabbed underwear and flew into the bathroom, rapidly reviewing which was the next fast train to London. With luck, she could still make it.

But only by the skin of her teeth, she admitted as she sank, panting, into a seat. And she wasn't her usual well-groomed self, either. There'd been no time to wash her hair, and she'd grabbed the first jacket and skirt she'd come to in the wardrobe.

As it was she was going to miss the start of the proceedings. She delved in her bag for her mobile phone and called Toby, but his phone was switched off—probably in deference to their father, who hated the things and complained bitterly if they went off in meetings, or anywhere else for that matter.

She looked restlessly at her watch. They would just about be assembling now, but there'd be coffee and biscuits first, so she might still have time to prime Toby before any potentially damaging revelations were made.

She took a cab from the station, thrusting money into the surprised driver's hand as she leapt out of the taxi and rushed into the company building. In the lift she tried to steady her flurried breathing as she combed her hair with her fingers.

Outside the boardroom, a secretary jumped to her feet. 'Miss Harrington—I mean, Mrs Destry—we weren't expecting you...'

'I can't think why not,' Paige said blandly, steaming past her and through the door.

Inside the room there was an atmosphere you could have cut with a knife. Her father was seated at the head of the table, with Nick facing him at its foot. The slim bearded man beside him must be Jake Allenby, she thought as she slid into an empty seat, and he must be taking the minutes—because no clerical staff were present. Not even Toby's secretary.

'I'm sorry I'm late,' she apologised charmingly, smiling round. 'My alarm didn't go off for some reason.'

She darted a lightning glance at Nick, expecting to see a glint of shared amusement in his eyes, but his face looked as if it had been hacked out of granite.

The lover who a few hours before had coaxed her body to extremes of delight might never have existed.

She looked down at the polished table, a faint curl of uneasiness in the pit of her stomach.

'We understood from Nicholas that you wouldn't be attending the meeting, my dear.' Her father sounded uncomfortable.

'I changed my mind,' she returned. 'May I have an agenda, please?'

Toby, who was sitting opposite her looking edgy, pushed a sheaf of papers towards her.

'We're on item three,' her father said. 'The interim financial report prepared by Mr—er—Allenby.'

Paige picked up her copy and opened it with hands that shook slightly.

'As I was saying before the interruption.' Nick's voice was as cold as stone too. 'The proper course of action is to launch a full internal investigation into all these gross irregularities, but news of it would almost certainly leak out, and the last thing we need is any more adverse publicity for Harringtons. As it is,' he added levelly, 'the company's reputation has suffered a blow from which it may never recover, and which Maitland Destry must share.'

'Isn't that rather an exaggeration?' Toby demanded aggressively. 'After all, we couldn't know the soil tests for Seagrove would be fudged. You take expert opinions on trust.'

'Indeed—when they *are* expert,' Nick drawled contemptuously. 'But the Seagrove development is only part of the problem, as the report makes clear. And the blame for that rests in this room.'

'Right.' Toby's laugh was shrill. 'So it's my head on the chopping block, is it? When I've been working night and day to save this company money.'

'How?' Nick asked. 'By putting third-rate kitchens and bathrooms into expensive houses? Rather a false economy, I'd have thought. Particularly when you've been charging the clients top dollar for them. Or did you think they wouldn't notice?'

'A misunderstanding with the suppliers,' Toby said airily. 'We've had problems with them in the past.'

'And yet you've continued to use them,' Nick said bitingly. 'A curious choice. But you'll continue as managing director for the time being. You have this disaster on the Seagrove site to sort out.'

'There will be additional funding from Maitland Destry?' Toby's voice was eager.

'This time, yes. On the understanding that this project, and all those in the pipeline, will be monitored by the bank's own people.'

'I really can't agree to that—' Toby began, but his father interrupted wearily.

'You don't have to,' he said. 'I've already done so.' He slapped the report with his hand. 'This—this is a nightmare.'

Toby sighed. 'Look, I cut a few corners. I admit it. But what the hell? Everyone makes mistakes.'

'Yes,' Nick said quietly. 'We're all fools at times.'

'So,' Toby said, 'things just carry on as normal.' He wasn't exactly smirking and rubbing his hands with glee, but he might as well have been, Paige thought despairingly. Couldn't he see how close he'd come to disaster?

'That's how it would appear,' Francis Harrington agreed. 'If there's no other business, I suggest we close the meeting.'

'There is one more thing.' Paige got to her feet. 'I'm resigning as head of public relations, as of today.'

'You can't do that,' Toby protested. 'Who's going to deal with the Seagrove people?'

'Nick's bringing in an outside company.' She glanced at him for confirmation, but he said nothing.

'Well, I think you should stay on,' Toby said pettishly. 'I've got used to dealing with you. It's—convenient.'

'But not for me,' Paige told him levelly. 'And, anyway, my mind's made up. I'm off the payroll. In fact, I'm going to clear out my desk and go home.'

'To do what, precisely?' His tone was sceptical.

This time she didn't look at Nick. She said, coolly and clearly, 'To have a baby.' And walked out, leaving a profound silence behind her.

There wasn't really a great deal to clear. She'd never tried to personalise the office in any way because she'd never felt it really belonged to her, so a jiffy bag took care of the contents of her desk drawers.

She worked slowly, waiting for Nick to come and find her after the bombshell she'd exploded.

He can hardly complain, she reassured herself. Not after last night. He wants a real marriage, and babies come with the territory.

She was trying to decide who the lucky recipient of her solitary spider plant should be when Toby walked in.

'Oh,' Paige said flatly. 'It's you.'

'Well, naturally. I had to come and congratulate you.'

'Thank you,' she said. 'But the announcement was a little premature.' Or perhaps not, she thought, her face warming slightly.

He waved a hand dismissively. 'I didn't mean that. You've been a very clever girl, Sis, and don't think it's not appreciated.' He gave a short laugh. 'My God, you certainly didn't waste any time.'

'I don't know what the hell you're talking about,' she said. 'But as you're here, I'd better warn you that Nick knows all about the scam you've been running with my expenses.'

He went pale. 'And just what is that supposed to mean?'

'Oh, don't lie,' she said scornfully. 'Luckily for you, he doesn't know you could always forge my signature. He thinks I've been helping myself to the money.'

He sat down heavily on the chair facing her desk. 'Thank God for that.'

'Forgive me if I don't say amen,' Paige told him bitterly. 'Whatever possessed you to do such a thing?'

He stared down at the carpet. 'It's Denise,' he muttered. 'She doesn't understand that we're going through a tough patch financially. The credit card bills alone are a nightmare.'

'Cut them up,' she said. 'Send them back and arrange to pay what you can each month.'

'I can't do that.' He sounded almost aggrieved. 'She'd leave me.'

'But she'll stick around if you go to jail?' Paige shook her head. 'You must be crazy.' She paused. 'You do have another option, of course. You could go to Nick—tell him everything, wipe the slate clean.'

'You have to be joking.' His expression was ugly. 'That would just make his triumph complete.'

'Does it really matter?' Her voice was weary. 'When he knows so much already? Your hands are hardly clean, Toby.'

He was watching her, eyes narrowed. 'There is another alternative, of course. You could always get me a rise in salary,' he said slowly. 'Call on those powers of persuasion you used so successfully last night.'

'What do you mean?'

'It's too late to play the innocent, my pet.' Toby was enjoying himself. 'I know Nick stayed at the cottage with you last night because his sidekick had it as a contact number. And he arrived here this morning looking like the cat who'd had the cream. It was clear to every guy in the building that someone had made him very, very happy in bed.'

'I didn't notice any obvious signs of joy in the meeting,' Paige said quietly, hot colour flooding her face.

He shrugged. 'Well, you have Snooper Allenby to thank for that. He dragged him into Dad's room for a few words in private, and that wiped the smile off your husband's face. But, even so, he didn't go back on his word. I'm still the managing director, and I have you to thank for it, my cherub. You're amazing, you know. All I had to do was point you in the right direction, and now he's twisted round your little finger.'

He laughed, as Paige stood frozen. Gazing past him.

'I hope the demon lover didn't make too many untoward demands,' he went on. 'What did you do—lie back and think of England?'

'No,' Nick said from the doorway behind him. 'Harringtons.'

Under any other circumstances, Paige thought detachedly, the expression on Toby's face would have been almost funny. As it was, she only wanted to die.

Her brother decided on belligerence. 'If you don't mind, I was having a private joke with my sister.'

'In between planning how to go on ripping off the company with her connivance?' Nick spoke quietly, but there was a note in his voice which made Paige shiver.

'Now just a minute...' Toby got to his feet.

'Get out of here,' Nick said. 'Before I do something I regret. And shut the door behind you.' he threw after his brother-in-law's ignominiously fleeing figure.

The door closed and husband and wife were alone, looking at each other.

Paige forced herself to move. To take a step forward towards him.

'Nick, you must listen to me...'

'You mean like you listened to me last night—pouring my heart out?' His glance flicked contempt at her. 'Telling you every maudlin, lovesick dream I ever had? I don't think so.'

She tried again, desperately. 'But you don't under-stand…'

'On the contrary, it's all perfectly clear. I had it straight from the horse's mouth—or do I mean another part of its anatomy?' His icy drawl seemed to flay the skin from her bones. 'You're a Harrington to your delectable fingertips, aren't you, darling? You'd do anything to protect your fam-ily. You might not lay down your life, but your body's a different proposition. And you had me fooled all along the line,' he went on bitterly. 'Tell me, do they teach you to fake your orgasms at the best schools?'

'Nick, you're angry, and I don't blame you. What you heard was terrible—shameful—but it wasn't true.'

His mouth twisted cynically. 'You mean your brother *didn't* suggest to you that I might let him off the hook in return for your sexual favours?'

'No,' she said huskily. 'I—can't pretend that.'

'I commend your honesty,' he said bitingly. 'Because he was stupid enough to telephone someone earlier—no doubt one of his partners in crime—and brag about it being all his idea. Jake was working in the adjoining office, checking his report.'

'But I refused.' She lifted her chin. 'I told him I'd have nothing to do with it and sent him away. You have to be-lieve me.'

He said slowly, 'If you'd told me last night that you hadn't been swindling money out of the company I'd have believed you. But you lied, Paige. And I knew it because I saw it in your eyes. But what I couldn't figure then was why you were taking the blame for something you hadn't done.'

He shook his head. 'I so desperately wanted you to be honest with me. I gave you every opportunity to explain.

Then Jake told me this morning he'd been comparing your actual signature to those on the expense claims and that there was something wrong—and I realised that you had to be shielding that worthless idiot.'

'And now you know why,' she said tiredly. 'Because while you might have forgiven me, you wouldn't have done the same for Toby. You might even have called the police in. I felt I had to protect Harringtons—just as you did in the boardroom today. And it went just as much against the grain with me, because I've had to accept that my brother is a crook, and that's not easy.' She paused. 'I was also concerned about the effect it might have on my father.'

'Your father's had his own suspicions for some time,' Nick said shortly. 'But he decided to share them with me. He's stronger than you think.'

Paige's laugh cracked in the middle. 'What a disappointment his children must be to him. One a thief and the other a liar—even if not a very good one.' She shook her head. 'It's ironic, isn't it? I tried to save Toby and ruined my own happiness instead.'

'Nothing can save Toby,' he said. 'There won't be a prosecution, for the company's sake, but his days here are numbered. Once the Seagrove disaster has been dealt with I'm recommending, with your father's approval, that Harringtons should be sold—probably to Winstanley UK. They're a good solid outfit, looking to expand.'

'Leaving you free to walk away?'

He shrugged. 'I should never have got involved with Harringtons in the first place. My judgement was—flawed. For obvious reasons.' He paused. 'But there'll be no place for Toby either. The whispers are already spreading about him.'

His mouth curled. 'I hope he's salted away his ill-gotten gains, because he could need them. And along with every-thing else he could lose that expensive wife of his.'

She said slowly, 'That's always been his greatest fear. And I never understood it before—how it was possible to love someone so much—to need them so desperately that you'd do anything—take any risk—in order to keep them. They say to understand is to forgive. I don't condone what my brother did, but for the first time I know why he did it.' She tried to smile and failed. 'Because that's how I love you, Nick. And now it seems that both Toby and I are going to end up alone.'

His face was taut, every bone stark under the tanned skin.

'Paige—you don't have to say these things.'

'Ah, but I do,' she said passionately. 'You've told me often that my eyes give me away if I'm lying. Well, look into them now, Nick, and see the whole truth. That you're my love and my life, and if I've lost you, then everything's gone. From that first moment I felt so much for you that I panicked—went into denial. I wanted you so badly, and yet I was convinced I was just the trade-off for a seat on the board.'

She took a sharp breath. 'We're both flawed, darling, and I don't care because I wouldn't change a thing about you. Mistakes and all, you're my man. Please—please let me be your woman.' Her voice was suddenly pleading, 'Oh, my love, don't send me back into the dark alone.'

He said harshly, 'Dear God, do you really think there's any way I could let you go? If I'd been in Toby's shoes I'd have done anything to keep you too. Because that's how it is—and always will be.'

There was a bubble of joy inside her, forcing its way to the surface, irradiating her whole being, making her want to sing, laugh and weep. But she kept her face solemn.

'Now that my desk is clear,' she said meditatively, 'I think I'll go back to the cottage. I haven't had much sleep in the last twenty-four hours,' she added. 'So I could do with an early night.'

Nick's face was equally grave as he consulted his watch. 'Don't you mean an early afternoon?'

'Yes,' she said. 'And evening. And the rest of our lives.'

He came to her then, and held her. His voice was suddenly rough. 'Do you know what you're taking on?'

Her eyes met his calmly, steadfastly. 'Yes, darling. I know. And we've wasted so much time already, I really can't wait any longer. I don't want our baby to be just wishful thinking.'

'I thought we might take a long weekend in Normandy,' he said. 'See if Grandmère will lend us that huge bed of hers for a second honeymoon.'

Paige's lips twitched. 'I'm sure she will,' she said. 'The French are so practical.'

'Oh,' he said, 'they have their dreams, too. And sometimes they come true.'

He stroked her hair back from her face with infinite tenderness. He said slowly, 'In fifty years' time I shall still be looking across a room filled with people and seeing only you.'

'And I,' Paige said softly, 'shall still be walking towards you.' She lifted her face for his kiss. 'Now take me home.'

The world's bestselling romance series.

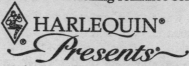

HARLEQUIN®
Presents

Seduction and Passion Guaranteed!

Introducing...
Jane Porter's exciting new series

**The Galván men: proud Argentinean aristocrats...
who've chosen American rebels as their brides!**

Don't miss

LAZARO'S REVENGE
by Jane Porter
Harlequin Presents #2304

Lazaro Herrera has vowed revenge
on Dante, his half brother, who
refuses to acknowledge his existence.
When Dante's sister-in-law Zoe
arrives in Argentina, it seems the
perfect opportunity. But the clash of
Zoe's blond and blue-eyed beauty
with his own smoldering dark looks
creates a sexual force so strong that
Lazaro's plan begins to fall apart....

On-sale February 2003

**Pick up a Harlequin Presents® novel and you will enter
a world of spine-tingling passion and provocative,
tantalizing romance!**

Available wherever Harlequin books are sold.

HARLEQUIN®
Makes any time special ®

Visit us at www.eHarlequin.com

HPGBJP

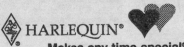

The world's bestselling romance series.

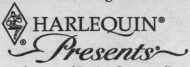

HARLEQUIN® *Presents*

Seduction and Passion Guaranteed!

He's impatient… He's impossible…
But he's absolutely irresistible!
He's…

HER ITALIAN BOSS

Two original short stories to celebrate Valentine's Day, by your favorite Presents authors, in one volume!

The Boss's Valentine by Lynne Graham

Poppy sent Santiano Aragone a Valentine card to cheer him up. Santiano responded by making love to her… and suddenly Poppy was expecting her boss's baby!

Rafael's Proposal by Kim Lawrence

Natalie's boss, Rafael Ransome, thought she couldn't be a single mom and do her job. But then he offered her a stunning career move—a Valentine's Day marriage proposal!

HER ITALIAN BOSS
Harlequin Presents, #2302
On-sale February 2003

Pick up a Harlequin Presents® novel and you will enter a world of spine-tingling passion and provocative, tantalizing romance!

Available wherever Harlequin books are sold.

HARLEQUIN®

Makes any time special ®

Visit us at www.eHarlequin.com

HPVCLG